Unwanted Attentions

Unwanted Attentions

K. K. Beck

Thorndike Press • Thorndike, Maine

Library of Congress Cataloging in Publication Data:

Beck, K. K.
    Unwanted attentions / K.K. Beck.
      p. cm.
    ISBN 0-89621-868-6 (lg. print : alk. paper)
    1. Large type books. I. Title.
  [PS3552.E248U59 1989]
  813'.54—dc19   89-4340
                                        CIP

All the characters and events portrayed in this story are
fictitious.

Large Print edition available in North America by arrangement
with Walker and Company.

Cover design by James B. Murray.

For Paul Sikora
with thanks for his legal expertise
and his flair for the dramatic

Prologue

In retrospect, it was amazing that Benjamin ever saw her at all. He hadn't wanted to go to the library and study. He'd had terrible headaches for days and days it seemed. He didn't know how long it had been that he'd lain in his dorm room with the shades drawn.

The school year had started out all right. He remembered the huge surge of relief he felt when his parents drove off, leaving him here. It would be great to be away from them with their constant nagging and picking on him. And his classes had been interesting at first, even though they were pretty hard. But lately it had all seemed so meaningless. Then the headaches started. Benjamin spent a lot of time in his room, reading spy novels. After the headaches came, he just spent a lot of time lying there. He was relieved when his roommate asked to be changed to another room. Benjamin wanted to be alone.

Then, one day, an important day in Benjamin's life, the twenty-eighth of April, 1973, he decided to get up and go out.

He vaguely remembered having been assigned a paper on Grover Cleveland in his American History class. He decided to go to the library and start researching.

Once there, however, he wondered whether it had been worthwhile getting out of bed. He felt listless and wandered aimlessly through the stacks.

And then, Benjamin Knapp looked down from the balcony that ran around the central reading room of the library. Below, in a book-lined oblong, he saw rows of tables dotted with piles of books and papers. He sighed wearily. Everyone sitting at those tables seemed so calm and businesslike, as if he or she belonged here. Benjamin knew he looked like them superficially, but he wasn't like them at all.

Who cared about Grover Cleveland? What did any of it matter? Before the headaches, and before he'd holed up with his spy novels, when his depression was just an itchy little feeling of despair that came and went, he'd tried to talk about it with someone.

The counselor at the health center said these depressions weren't anything special. Lots of freshmen got them. It would probably go away. Benjamin knew it would never go away. He would spend the rest of his life in the grip of this numbing sadness.

The room was silent, except for the sounds of birds chirping idiotically outside the high windows and the flick of the occasional turned page. Then Benjamin saw her. She was tall and lanky, sitting a little tomboyishly, her chair tipped back from the table, her long legs in blue jeans stretched out beneath it. She was wearing a Stanford sweatshirt and a little string of beads around one wrist.

She pushed back her heavy dark blonde hair and tucked it behind an ear. Benjamin watched, fascinated. She pushed up one sleeve of the sweatshirt and leaned forward, her smooth face frowning over the page of her book. Benjamin felt an explosion in his chest and grabbed the balcony railing to compensate for his dizziness. He didn't know who she was, but he would find out. Because this was it — love at first sight — and she would be his, now and forever.

The burden of sadness left him suddenly, as if some devil that had held onto him with its tenacious claws had suddenly lost its grip. Benjamin felt alive again. Alive, and full of purpose. He knew he'd write letters and poems to her. Someday he'd show them all to her. He would wait for the right time and place. Their meeting, like everything else about their lives, must be perfect. It was all meant to be.

9

He'd asked for a sign and he had received it. The universe wasn't against him after all. He'd thought he was just some piece of garbage that the universe meant to chew up and spit out, but he was wrong. There *was* a place for him. A very special place.

God, he'd been so unhappy. But that was just because his life wasn't complete without her. Now his life could really start. With this woman as part of it — as part of him — and the first thing he had to do was find out her name, which had been easier than he thought.

He'd followed her back to the dorm that afternoon. A few questions from the girl at the desk, and he had a name. Rebecca. Rebecca Kendall. It hadn't taken much longer to learn her schedule and who her friends were. He'd simply followed her some more — at a distance. There were plenty of times he'd wanted to approach her and tell her about them, but he'd known better. He had to wait. Bide his time. Make it perfect.

A girl in her dorm was in one of his classes. He'd been skipping most of his classes lately to keep his eye on Rebecca, but he started going to Geology and made friends with Wendy. She was an unattractive girl with a glowering expression and thick legs. He invited her for coffee and she seemed pleased.

Soon, he and Wendy were meeting for

lunch at the cafeteria and going to movies on campus. He hated being with Wendy when he should have been with Rebecca, but it had to be done.

Finally, he realized his hard work had been worth it. Benjamin's parents had always told him he never could apply himself. They were so wrong. After all, he got into Stanford, didn't he? And now he was setting out to win something he really wanted.

He was waiting for Wendy in the lounge of Rebecca's dorm. They were going to the library to study. Not that Benjamin was studying much lately. He saw a friend of Rebecca's talking on the phone in one of the booths down the hall. He knew from eavesdropping that her name was Casey. She had the door to the booth open, so he went over to where she stood. Maybe he'd learn something.

She was a careless-looking girl with long dark hair and too much makeup, definitely not the sort Rebecca should have for a friend, he thought with disapproval. She was also loud, as usual.

"Yeah, it should be a great party," she was saying. "It's at Mel Bentley's house. He's an associate professor, and he invited some of his students. But the fabulous thing is, I know Carl daSilva's going. It's the first chance I'll really have to talk to him."

11

Benjamin frowned. And listened.

Casey was laughing now. "Believe me, if I get my way, he won't have a chance. I'm going to make a move. You should see this guy. He's just gorgeous." She paused. "I think I'll take Rebecca Kendall with me. Just in case I don't nail Carl, I can have someone to talk to. She's really very sweet. And she's so gorgeous, he's bound to notice us when we come in." There was another pause. "I doubt it. Cause *I'm* the one who's going to make the move. Rebecca isn't into the sexual revolution like I am." She laughed again. "Let's face it. Guys just don't know how to say no."

Benjamin kept his study date with Wendy. In the library he went over to the faculty directory and looked up Associate Professor Melvin Bentley. He smiled reassuringly at Wendy, bent over her books at one of the long tables as he researched. Then he consulted the local phone book. Five minutes later, he went to a phone booth outside the library and called Bentley's number. A woman answered.

"Hello," said Benjamin. "I'm a student of Dr. Bentley's and he's invited me to a party you're giving." He chuckled a little. "I'm really embarrassed because I forgot the date."

"Oh," said the woman. "It's Friday night."

Benjamin didn't say anything. Friday night.

Friday night would be the beginning.

"Would you like to talk to my husband?" asked the woman, obviously taken aback by the moment of silence.

"No, that's okay," said Benjamin. "Sorry to bother you. I'll see you later."

"Do you have the address?" said the woman. He repeated the address in the phone book.

"That's right," she replied.

He hung up and leaned against the booth. He was glad the professor hadn't answered, but he'd been ready if that had happened. He'd have used the name he heard Casey talking about. Carl daSilva. He had hoped the professor wouldn't notice his voice was different.

Benjamin chided himself. He'd taken a risk. What he should have done was check out Dr. Bentley's schedule and call when he was teaching. He'd been hasty because he was so anxious, but that was no excuse. Any operation should be well thought out to the last detail. Benjamin knew that from his vast reading of spy novels.

Well, he thought, there's no reason to be so hard on myself. After Friday, everything will be okay.

Benjamin went back into the library. He told a slightly surprised Wendy that he had a stomachache and was going home. "I'll walk you back to your dorm," he said. Benjamin felt a little guilty about Wendy. Not very guilty, just a little. Besides, he didn't want her calling and bothering him. So he explained it to her at the door to Roble Hall.

"We'd better not see each other any more, Wendy," he said. "I'm engaged to someone else. She probably wouldn't want me to spend so much time with another woman."

1

"Look at us," thought Rebecca. "We look like people in a commercial."

She had caught her reflection and Philip's in the lobby mirror as they waited for the elevator in her building. It was an undeniably attractive picture. They were both tall, healthy looking, and in their mid-thirties. He was in black tie. She was wearing green taffeta, green to match her new emerald ring, and cut narrow in the torso and stiff and flaring in the skirt. Her dark blonde hair was twisted up, emphasizing her chiseled profile.

Philip's hands rested on her bare shoulders. He was saved from being too handsome by the thin tortoiseshell glasses.

He kissed her, and she wished she hadn't caught that glimpse of them in the mirror. Life wasn't like commercials. This couldn't be real life and she couldn't be this happy. She thought of sharing this disquieting thought. The elevator bell chimed softly, and she smiled at him as they went in. Why share a thought like that after such a perfect evening?

Her apartment was a rather austere place in pale, neutral colors, with the transient look of all the apartments she'd ever lived in. Philip went to the refrigerator, where he'd put a bottle of champagne earlier. Rebecca kicked off her shoes and stretched out on the sofa.

"Happy?" called out Philip from the kitchen.

She smiled lazily. "Yes," she said.

"Did you like my friends?"

"Delightful," she replied. "Good-hearted and generous."

He came into the living room with two crystal flutes in one hand, the bottle in the other. He sat down on the floor next to her and began twisting the wire on the champagne cork.

"It was awfully nice of them to have a party for us," Rebecca continued. "And what a party! Fabulous food. A fashionable caterer. Dancing to live music. I can't get used to such luxury. I'm afraid we can't expect the same from my friends. Academics run more to wine and cheese parties."

"I know," he said, punctuated by the pop of the champagne cork. "And lots of Harris tweed."

She reached out and touched his shoulder. "I worried about that, you know," she said. "That your friends would all be too glitzy and

16

you'd think mine were too dull."

He handed her a glass. "You worry too much. We're marrying each other. Not our friends."

With a rustling of green taffeta, she sat up, tucking her feet under her on the sofa so she could sip her champagne. He sat next to her and put his arm around her.

"You're so calm," she said. "Aren't you just the tiniest bit jittery?"

"No. Why should I be? People get married all the time."

"I know. But they used to do it when they were young and foolish and full of hormones. They didn't think about it so much. My mother always said, 'You'll know when you meet the right person.' It used to be an act of faith."

He frowned. "We're both intelligent people with some experience of life. We aren't going to rush into anything without thinking it through."

"You're right, of course," she said.

"Now will you lighten up, Dr. Kendall?" He kissed her cheek. "If you want to write a paper about modern marriage customs, go ahead. But I don't want you to analyze our relationship in that detached way."

She didn't bother to tell him that as a history professor, modern marriage customs weren't part of her field of study. He seemed to assume her scholarly pursuits knew no bounds.

"You know," she said slowly, "when I was in the lobby and we were standing in front of the elevator, I caught a glimpse of us. I thought we looked like we were in a commercial."

"Yeah?" He smiled. "I hope it was for some upscale product."

"Definitely." She was relieved she'd mentioned it to him. His reaction was different from hers, probably healthier. "That dress is fabulous," he added.

"I know. Thanks for helping me pick it out." She paused. "Philip, be honest. Did you want to come with me to find a dress for this party tonight because you thought I'd get something drab like a college professor might wear?"

"Well, the thought did cross my mind." He looked a little worried. "What's the matter? Do you think I was being pushy?"

"No. I was touched, and I love this dress. It makes me feel like Audrey Hepburn. She was my favorite movie star when I was a kid, and this is definitely an Audrey Hepburn dress." Rebecca hesitated. "I've never bought clothes with a man before. In fact, there are lots of things I haven't done with a man."

"We're really very nice once you get used to us."

She embraced him. "Oh, Philip, until I met you, I didn't realize how lonely I've been."

"I know," he said. "Me too. But I didn't tell you why I wanted you to have that dress, besides the fact that it looks terrific on you."

"Why?"

"Because that's a dress for a wife."

"What do you mean?"

He reached behind her and ran his hand down her spine and the long row of tiny covered buttons there. "No way in hell you could get in and out of this dress without someone to help you."

Marriage, she had always thought, was a state one must approach whole. It was wrong to need a man — to need his admiration or to need him to change a tire or get up in the night because of a noise downstairs — a banging shutter or mysterious creak.

But Philip had changed her. Slowly, and with a sense of relief, she'd decided it wasn't so terrible to need someone. Life didn't have to be led alone and bravely, and he would need her as much as she needed him.

It hadn't been easy to surrender emotional habits of a lifetime. She had felt, somehow, that she was giving up part of herself. But slowly she realized the part she was giving up was lonely and a little bitter.

So she said yes, and there was a great sense of relief. She could look at babies and little children without feeling she had to pull back emotionally. She let down her guard and allowed herself to be loved.

That had been the hardest part. Being loved intensely frightened her. There was a logical explanation for that, of course. She hated to believe that Benjamin Knapp had had the power to form her personality, but she knew he did. His sickness had made her wary. She'd never told Philip about that. She hadn't wanted to ruin everything, but she wondered sometimes if she should.

"What are you thinking about?" said Philip now. "You think too much. I can almost see your brain racing behind that deceptively calm face."

She was serious all of a sudden. "Philip, do you think we should tell each other everything? About our pasts?"

"Absolutely not!" said Philip. "What a terrible idea." He looked, as usual, amused at her seriousness. "Ann Landers even says so," he added.

Rebecca was silent.

"Anything in particular you had in mind?" he said. "Insanity in the family?"

20

"You're close," she said. "Benjamin wasn't family, but he was insane."

"Benjamin? Some guy from your past. I don't want to hear about it." He shook his head. "I can't believe this conversation. We're both old enough to have had other people in our lives. And if you expect me to tell you about . . . " He frowned. "Wait a minute. Did you say Benjamin?"

"Never mind," she said.

What had possessed her to bring it up now? Was she trying to destroy everything?

"Benjamin Knapp, by any chance?"

She sat bolt upright, her eyes wide.

Philip reached into his jacket pocket.

"I got this, just before I left. I thought it was some kind of joke. I meant to ask you about it." He handed her a telegram.

YOU MUST NOT MARRY REBECCA. SHE IS MINE. WE HAVE BEEN ENGAGED FOR YEARS AND SHE KNOWS IT. SHE IS LIVING A LIE, FOR SHE KNOWS SHE IS MINE AND I AM HERS. IF SHE DE-NIES IT, SHE IS ONLY PUTTING OFF THE MOMENT OF RECKON-ING. YOU MUST NEVER SEE HER AGAIN. I FORBID IT. BENJAMIN KNAPP.

21

"It's not a joke," she said simply. "How could you have thought so?"

"It seemed like one to me. It's so melodramatic. I figured it was one of my crazy friends."

A feeling of oppression came over her. "I thought it was all over," she said.

"What do you mean? Were you engaged to this guy?"

"No! It's hard to grasp, I know. He's completely mad. He thinks he's in love with me. Philip, this guy has been stalking me for years. Ever since I was eighteen."

Philip's handsome face clouded over. He looked genuinely puzzled. She felt a stab of impatience with him. This was always so hard to explain, and she'd thought it was over.

"You mean he's your old high school sweetheart or something?" Philip was looking at the telegram.

"No. For some reason that I've tried to figure out and never have, he's obsessed with me."

"Well what did you do to get him all riled up like that?"

She felt a surge of anger. "Will you *listen?* It's nothing I did. I didn't do anything. For years I thought it was somehow my fault, but it's not. It's not my fault." She realized she was shouting.

2

In May of 1973, Rebecca Kendall stood before the long mirror on the back of her dorm room door and dressed to go to a party. It was an off-campus party, at the house of a junior faculty member and his wife. Most of the people there would be graduate students. Rebecca was pleased and excited.

She dressed carefully. She wanted to look terrific, but casual, as if she hadn't tried too hard. She wore a Mexican peasant dress, white cotton with embroidered flowers around the neck, and a pair of sandals. Her long hair hung straight from a center part. She put on long silver earrings from India and shook her hair free. Maybe, she thought, as she always did at eighteen, she would meet some fabulous guy at this party.

She'd thought a lot about that spring evening in the next fifteen years. Much of it seemed so clear. The anticipation she'd felt while getting ready, for instance. It was a feeling no grown woman could ever really have because a grown woman has a past that, to an extent, dictates her future. A girl has nothing but a future — mysterious, exhilarating, terrifyng.

Back then, Rebecca Kendall had consulted the I Ching and the tarot with a feverish suspense. Any new venture, no matter how small — like this party in the Los Altos Hills above Stanford — seemed fraught with possibilities. Maybe she'd meet someone there who would change everything.

The evening ended badly. As badly as any evening ever had again. But there was one thing she never understood. Why did the first part of the evening live in her memory as such a shimmering, beautiful time? Those few hours in that overgrown, neglected garden, behind a low house covered with bougainvillea and honeysuckle, lingered like some tantalizing childhood dream.

The taste of the wine punch with slices of lemon floating in it — some cheap wine heavily disguised, she realized now. The sound of fat velvety bees humming lazily in the bougainvillea and of crickets somewhere beyond. The air on her bare arms and legs, cooling as dusk fell and shadows stretched out over the lawn. The clarity of the memory gave those hours the sad beauty of something lost forever. Innocence, she supposed.

She had gone there with her friend Casey in Casey's car. The host was a thin, intense man, a sociologist. Casey was one of his students. His wife — Rebecca had long ago forgotten their names — was pregnant, a rather unusual condition in those days. She was round and rosy. Rebecca remembered an earnest conversation with her about motherhood. The woman already had a child of about two, a blond boy with corkscrew curls who tottered around the garden in his pajamas.

And there was Casey's friend. Rebecca had spotted him first. He was brooding and Byronic looking. Dark, with a cleft chin and shining brown eyes. Someone said his name was Carl. Rebecca had smiled at him, given him sidelong glances while she was talking to other people. He'd noticed her too. But before she had a chance to talk to him, he and Casey were dancing. Rebecca felt a horrible pang and tried to will him to forget about Casey and come to her side. But he never did. He stayed with Casey the whole evening.

She talked, she laughed, she danced. She drank more wine. She'd almost forgotten her disappointment when Casey and Carl came up to her.

Casey looked apologetic. "Listen, if it's okay with you, we're going to take off now. This is Carl."

Carl, his arm around Casey, gave Rebecca a cool look of appraisal with more than a little smugness about it. "Hi, Rebecca," he said seductively.

"But it's okay," said Casey. "I've got a ride for you back to campus."

"I guess it'll have to be okay," said Rebecca, rather coldly.

Casey shook free of Carl and took Rebecca aside, whispering desperately. "Listen, I've got to go. I've been crazy about this guy all quarter. I can't believe we're together. Aren't you happy for me? Hey, I'd do it for you."

"It's okay," said Rebecca with a frown.

She glanced over at Carl. He looked older. In his mid-twenties at least. He was giving the girls an amused smile. Rebecca felt young and silly.

"No problem," she said airily, forcing a smile.

"Thanks," said Casey, squeezing her arm. "I mean it." She gazed blearily back at Carl.

"Wait!" said Rebecca, after they'd started to leave. "Where's my ride?"

"Oh," said Casey, looking distracted, as Carl was massaging her back languorously. "That guy over there. His name's Benjamin."

Rebecca looked in the direction Casey indicated. A young man stood there, more clean-cut than the rest of the people at the party, but presentable and actually rather sweet looking. Rebecca felt reassured, but slightly disappointed. As smug and sleazy as Carl seemed, he was undeniably attractive. Rebecca at eighteen conceded him the right to be smug and sleazy, and Benjamin looked like kind of a jerk. She didn't remember ever seeing him before. But he'd seen her.

3

Rebecca tried to suppress her irritation at Philip's confusion. It wasn't really his fault, she knew, but why couldn't he just shut up and listen? To cover her annoyance, she disentangled herself from his arms and got up from the sofa.

"I'll make coffee," she said. "It's a long story."

She tried to make it short. She told him very quickly about Benjamin's seeing her that day in the library, about how he arranged to be at the party, and how, when Casey and Carl decided to leave, he managed to pop into place and offer her a ride back to campus.

She made coffee with Philip lounging against the kitchen counter, his jacket off now, his white shirt gleaming against his light tan. She began to tell him about the ride she and Benjamin took that night. Again, she tried to keep it concise and unemotional, but even as her words came out in flat, dead tones, she remembered it all vividly. It was as if her memories raced along ahead and her narration, simple and spare, came from another part of her mind entirely.

"Any time you're ready just let me know," Benjamin had said.

He actually had rather a sweet smile. Rebecca felt guilty that she'd dismissed him as a jerk. It was nice of him to offer her a ride and to tell her that any time she wanted to leave, he would. She gave him a smile in return, and his face relaxed. The sweet smile blossomed into an unguarded, wide and happy one.

He looked incredibly young, even younger than the eighteen he was then. His skin was fresh and rosy. It didn't look like he shaved. And he was tall and kind of gangly, with knobby wrists and large hands at the end of long, thin arms. His hair was like a child's, fine and limp and sandy, cut shorter than was fashionable with a cowlick that sent the surrounding hair up in points. His eyes were light blue — intelligent-looking eyes with pale lashes and a steady, intense gaze that she hadn't noticed until later. Why hadn't she noticed that gaze then?

Rebecca shrugged. "It's up to you," she said. "I really appreciate your giving me a ride."

"No problem," he said.

"You look kind of familiar," she continued.

"You aren't in any of my classes, are you?"

"No," he said firmly. "I'm not." She should have noticed that too. How could he have known with such certainty? Some of their lecture classes were huge.

"I know," Rebecca had said then, "I've seen you with Wendy. From my dorm."

He frowned. "She's just a friend," he murmured.

That was the third sign she ignored. Nothing important, just a tiny signal, a response that was just a little odd (why would he feel compelled to tell her Wendy was just a friend?), but together they should have made a picture of someone slightly off center. Instead, Rebecca had taken the fact that he knew Wendy from her dorm — a quiet, studious girl down the hall — as a sign that he was okay.

"Well, listen," she said. "If you don't mind, I'd like to go now." She looked around at the gathering. Carl's leaving with Casey had taken the festive edge off things. The party that had been fraught with exciting possibilities now seemed empty and used up. The garden, the heavy scent of flowers barely visible in the dark, the coolness that came from the dampening grass, and the sky lit with stars of special brightness up here in the hills all suddenly seemed oppressive and full of a gloomy kind of beauty.

They had a little trouble finding his beige VW in the dark. In the background they heard the laughter and conversation and music from the party. Closer at hand, they heard crickets and Rebecca's sandaled feet crunching along the gravel. A long row of cars was parked outside the professor's house, wedged between the curving asphalt street and the ditch full of grass and dusty earth that ran alongside. There were no sidewalks up here in the hills, and no storm drains either.

She went around to the passenger side, expecting Benjamin to open the door from the inside if it was locked. Instead, he came around with her. She started to slip. The car was parked right next to the ditch and she stepped on the edge of it. One of her feet began to slide downward in a flurry of dry earth. Benjamin took her arm and helped her back up and into the car. She recoiled from his touch. It was so unexpected, and his hand and forearm were hot and a little damp. She felt his hot breath on her cheek for just an instant.

The inside of the VW was immaculate. She'd had a vague impression of him as fastidious, and it was squeaky clean here. The car interior even had the piney smell of some cleaning preparation.

Benjamin put the car in gear, and they drove off. He did something then that startled

31

her. He laughed. And then he turned to her and said "Rebecca." She wasn't sure why he'd laughed, but she assumed he repeated her name because he wasn't sure what it was.

"That's right," she said. "Rebecca Kendall. And you're Benjamin, right?"

"Benjamin Knapp. We have the same last initial."

Boy, he makes terrible small talk, she thought. Then she noticed how fast he was driving. It seemed out of character. He was racing through the curved suburban streets toward the west, away from the Bay and toward the ocean and the Skyline Highway, the main route across the high, uninhabited ridge of the San Francisco peninsula.

"You're going Skyline?" she said, puzzled. She and Casey had come up from the El Camino, through the Los Altos Hills.

"Isn't it a fabulous night?" he said. He cranked open the sun roof. "Look at those stars!"

There was something too enthusiastic about his voice — something out of control and manic.

"Yes, lovely," she said calmly.

He ran a stop sign at the entrance to Skyline, careening out of the Los Altos Hills and onto the dune-lined highway. It was nearly deserted, so there wasn't anything especially dangerous about the maneuver, but Rebecca was unsettled. She wondered how much Benjamin Knapp had had to drink at the party. Or maybe he was high on grass. There'd been plenty of that wafting around the garden.

"This has got to be the most beautiful road in the world," Benjamin said.

"It's kind of dark," said Rebecca nervously.

Actually, she could see. There was a full moon, and here, away from lights, the stars were vivid. There were more of them than she ever remembered seeing, and they appeared to be arranged in huge waving bands. They lit up the sky and below, past the dunes, they lit up the beach. As Benjamin's VW plowed down the highway, they saw a changing vista of beach, sometimes a long sandy stretch, then a jutting point and another cove. The beach would disappear for a moment behind the dunes, then it would emerge spectacularly into view.

The Pacific rolled in, glassy sheets of shallow waves crisscrossing each other as they surged into round coves across shiny wet sand, then cascaded into swirls and eddies among the outcroppings of dark, kelp-covered rocks. Even here, well above the beach, they could hear the roar of the ocean.

Rebecca knew he was driving too fast. She was sure now that he was high on something,

33

but she was still overwhelmed by the ocean below them. The sheer force of it blotted out any concerns she might have had about Benjamin Knapp at that point.

"You love it, don't you?" he said, turning to look at her face.

"Yes. It's gorgeous. But keep your eyes on the road, and slow down." She knew she sounded severe, so she smiled at him reassuringly.

"Oh, God, Rebecca, how can I keep my eyes off you," he said exuberantly.

"What!" She was startled. She assumed he was joking, or flirting in some heavy-handed way. He must be drunk.

She debated whether she should try to take over the driving. She didn't want to set him off. He seemed fairly emotional — elated. But maybe a wrong word would turn him nasty. Who could tell? Still, the vision of that tiny VW rolling over one of the bluffs down toward the ocean, bouncing off rocks, and landing crumpled on the sand terrified her.

"How about if I drive," she said. "Did you have a lot of wine at the party?"

He slowed down a little and gave her a pinched look. "I don't drink," he said.

"Well maybe you smoked some . . ."

"I don't take drugs, either," he said primly. "I want you to know that about me. I'm abso-

34

lutely pure. I noticed you were drinking wine at that party. I didn't like that. It's not right. We both need to keep ourselves healthy and pure, free of any extraneous influences."

"What are you talking about?" she demanded, and regretted it as soon as she did.

The young man at the wheel was obviously crazy.

"I'm talking about us," he said simply.

He pulled the car off the road onto a track of tar and gravel that led to a bluff overlooking the ocean. He downshifted roughly, scraping the gears, and jerked the car forward, burying its front wheels in sand. He pulled up the hand brake between their bucket seats with a ratchety sound and turned to face her.

"I'm sorry, Rebecca, I meant to go more slowly, but I feel so strongly about us, I just assumed you felt the same way. Tell me honestly. Don't you feel something between us? Something very special?"

She pulled away from him, smashing herself against the door. She could feel the discomfort of the door handle and the cool of the window glass against her back as she looked at him with terror and then tried to hide that look. She mustn't let him know she was frightened, just as you mustn't let a dog smell your fear. Still, Benjamin Knapp struck her less as a vicious, snarling dog than as an overexuberant puppy, the kind that would knock you down with big paws and slobber all over your face.

"Well, Benjamin," she began, "I don't really know you that well. Maybe if we got a chance to know each other — " If only she could get him to take her home, she'd be rid of him forever. Until then, she'd promise anything. "I'm very tired now," she said. "I want to go home."

"You're frightened," he said solicitously. He stroked her arm, then withdrew his hand hastily. "I don't want to frighten you. You'll just have to learn to trust me. I'd never hurt you."

"I'm sure you wouldn't," she said. If only she could keep up this conversational tone. He was obviously too crazy to know that what he was saying made no sense at all. But if she just maintained this reassuring, bland tone, she felt sure she'd be safe.

"Oh, I *might* hurt you. Just a little," he said now. "If you didn't do what you were supposed to do. But that wouldn't happen. Because you're the perfect girl, Rebecca."

She said nothing to this. For the first time she felt a real hopeless, sinking feeling. She had a horrifying sense that there was nothing to do now but wait. Wait and see what it was he wanted. She hoped it wasn't rape. She'd fight if it was rape, she decided, but anything less she'd endure until she could get to safety.

"I don't understand — ," she began helplessly. Her hands were in fists, her body stiff and defensive.

Benjamin buried his face in his hands for a moment. "Sometimes I have a hard time expressing myself," he said through his fingers.

She felt safe for that fraction of a second when his head was down. Then it was up again, those pale blue eyes staring at her intensely.

"I've never told a girl this before, Rebecca," he began rather formally. "But I love you. I've loved you ever since I first saw you."

"Tonight?" she asked incredulously. "At the party?"

He waved his hand dismissively. "No, not there. I only went because I knew you'd be there."

He must have noticed the chilling effect this information had on her, because he added, "That's right. I overheard your friend Casey talking about it on the phone in your dorm. She said she'd be coming with you. I know a lot about you, Rebecca. I've been watching you." He paused, ignoring her wide-eyed look. "Do you believe in love at first sight?" he said, sounding puzzled. "I'd heard about it, but until I saw you in the library — "

"You saw me in the library," she repeated.

"That's right. You know the balcony that runs around the main reading room? I was just standing there, and I looked down, and I just knew, Rebecca." He frowned. "I'm kind of surprised you don't feel the same way."

"Well I don't know, Benjamin, it's just that, well, until tonight I never knew you existed."

She realized almost instantly that it was the wrong thing to say.

He glowered at her. "Well I do exist. And one day, I'll be central to your existence too. Do you understand that? You're the one for me. And I'm the one for you."

"It might take me some time to — "

"Let's go for a walk on the beach, Rebecca."

"But it's so cold," she began. They were all alone up here on the bluff, but at least the road was nearby. On the beach anything could happen to her. No one would ever know.

"You must take me back to campus," she said in a firm, low voice. "I want to go home."

"Not until we get a few things straightened out," he said. "We're going for a walk."

"No." She was practically shouting. How dare this little creep tell her what to do? "Listen," she said, "I'm sorry if you have some sort of crush on me. But I don't know

38

you, and I don't want to. I want you to take me home. People know we left that party together, so there's no point in your trying anything. You'll just get caught."

"Shut up," he said softly. Then he struck her hard across the face.

Her head snapped violently, and her eyes felt loose, as if they were rolling around in their sockets like marbles. Tears sprang up but she found herself striking him back anyway, slapping him as hard as he'd slapped her. His head didn't bounce like hers had. He just kept staring at her as a red mark rose on his light skin. He looked genuinely confused.

"Take me home," she screamed.

"Oh, Rebecca," he said softly. "Our first fight. I'm so sorry."

She raised her hand to slap him again. This time she wanted his head to knock against the window like hers had. Instead, he grabbed her wrist as it made its arc. His hands seemed huge. She twisted and writhed trying to get her hand free but he held on.

"You're hurting me."

"This is all wrong," he said in a whiny voice, still holding on to her wrist. "It isn't how I planned it."

"That's because you never stopped to think about me and my feelings. You can't plan for another person," she said. "Let go of me."

He turned and stared at his hand encircling her wrist, straining against her struggling, his knuckles white and raised. He seemed startled by the sight and let go.

"Just take a short walk with me on the beach, Rebecca," he said. "It's what I imagined. Our walking together on the beach. Hand in hand. Talking about the future."

"All right," she said. She had remembered that he'd helped her into the car, running around and opening the door for her like a real little gentleman. If he did the same thing now, running around and opening her door, she'd have a moment alone. And if he left the keys in the car . . .

She tried not to look at the ignition. She planned it so that when he was at the farthest point from the two doors she'd lock them. Then she'd drive away. He had struck her. She had no choice.

Staring straight ahead, she saw the silver glimmer of the keys dangling in the ignition. She heard him open his door. He slid out his side. She tried to wait. It was hard. She wanted to lock the doors and start the car right away, but she had to give herself her best shot.

She turned and saw him walking around the car. She didn't dare take the time to lock the doors. She had to get out of here right now. She reached out for the keys, felt them with the tips of her fingers, prepared to move awkwardly over the gear shift lever onto the driver's seat, when he came back.

He opened the door and leaned in, snatching the keys. "I almost left the keys in the ignition," he said. "That's not like me."

She wondered if he knew she'd meant to get away. There seemed to be no guile in his voice. She watched him slip the keys into his shirt pocket and settled back into the passenger seat. There was no point locking the doors now. He had the keys. But she felt like doing it anyway. Just for a minute, she'd be safe. She imagined herself struggling to hold down the door button, watching his face almost next to hers through the window. It would never work.

Whistling as if there were nothing the matter at all, he went around the car and opened her door.

"I can't go down on the beach with you," she said. "I can't." She felt as if she were beginning to cry.

"But you said you would," he said, frowning. "I told you. This is the way I planned it."

"Please, please," she said. "Take me back to campus. I'm cold and miserable. I have to get back." Suddenly she thought of her parents. She thought of the times she'd laughed at them for being so protective. Now all she wanted was her mother and father.

He took her hand and pulled her from the car. She screamed and twisted in his grasp.

"Stop it!" he shouted, and she noted with some satisfaction that there was an edge of panic in his voice. He wasn't completely sure of his ability to control her. Facing her, he wrapped his arms around her and held her in a big hug, pinning her arms against her body. "What's the matter with you?" he demanded. "I just wanted to take a nice walk on the beach."

"But I don't!" she shouted back.

"If you'd just understand what you're supposed to do," he said, obviously frustrated.

He was taller than she had thought — half a head taller than she was — so she was able to duck her head, then slam it up against his jaw from below. He groaned and let go.

In that moment, she raked her fingernails down his face, feeling the flesh beneath them and surprising herself by the force with which she tore at his skin. He gave a little cry, and she turned and ran to the road.

She knew it was hopeless, but she had to try. She'd never run so hard in her life, willing her legs to pump hard, stretching them so each step covered as much ground as possible. Her heart was pounding in her chest.

She heard him behind her but she kept on, even when she felt his hand reach out and touch her shoulder. She ran down the rough short path and across the gravel to the highway. Something about reaching the blacktop made her feel safer. She was wearing that white dress. She'd be spotted if anything came along.

In the distance were headlights coming toward them, two long beams jutting out and getting closer. It was cooler now, and wisps of fog were rolling in. She saw fog swirling in front of those approaching headlights. She jumped and waved while the car kept coming, but it was still a hundred yards or so off when Benjamin caught up with her and began to drag her back.

She fought him all the way, but he kept pulling her along, groaning with exertion. When the car reached them, they were almost all the way off the road. She heard the angry sound of the horn and was vaguely aware of the car swerving as he pulled her down into the drainage ditch.

He lay on top of her, pushing her face into gravel and rough, dried grass. He seemed to be catching his breath, his body heaved slightly, then became racked with shuddering. For a ghastly moment she thought he might be sexually excited, then she realized he was sobbing.

"You're crushing me," she said angrily. "Get off!"

He rolled off and sat there slumped over, his face red and blotchy from crying. She stared at him with fascination. He looked so weak and defeated now. She inspected her knees and elbows for scratches and brushed dirt and gravel out of the abrasions there.

"This isn't how it was supposed to be," he said, tears coursing down his cheeks. The way his moods could swing back and forth terrified her, but she preferred to see him helpless like this.

"Let's go back to campus," she said gently, even though she wanted to slap him, kick him, stomp on him. "We can talk in the morning."

"No," he said, wiping his eyes with his hands, leaving smudgy streaks on his childish face. "I want to take that walk on the beach."

"Out of the question!" she snapped. "We've got to get back."

"We're taking that walk."

Suddenly she was staring at the knife he held an inch from her face. It looked like her father's hunting knife, a blade of six inches or so, straight along one edge, and serrated along part of the other before it became a sharp point. She imagined it had come from the pocket of his windbreaker.

She stood, fighting the nausea rising in her throat. He took her arm and led her down the path. It was dark. She had no idea where the knife was. But his hand was wrapped firmly around her upper arm.

They walked past the car and down the soft, sandy path through the dunes. It was like walking in snow. Her feet sank into the cool sand as she went. It was a steep descent, so she almost fell forward a few times, but he never let go of her.

When they got to the bottom, the ocean was loud, a steady roar. He led her to the part of the beach that was wet and firm underfoot, where walking was easier. "Now," he said. "Let's hold hands." He took her hand. She didn't resist, but she made sure her hand felt limp and awful in his. He didn't seem to notice.

They walked together in silence, the water rushing in and sucking at their feet. Some trick of the moonlight had given a phosphorescent glaze to the flat expanse of wet sand. Fog came in, floating in phantomlike patches about the water and onto land.

She didn't dare speak. Who knew what might set him off? She remained silent, zombielike, telling herself that if she became completely passive he'd never use the knife, and suppressing her thoughts of what the worst she could expect would be.

Finally, he turned to her. "We don't really need to talk, do we?" he said dreamily. "When you're in love, communication happens on another level."

She just stared at him.

He looked pale in the moonlight, but quite happy, almost radiant, with a dreamy expression.

"Rebecca," he began solemnly, "I'm afraid this evening hasn't gone exactly as it was meant to. First dates can be a little awkward."

Again, she just stared at him.

He took the knife out of his pocket again, and still holding her hand he held it up to her. "I don't want you to think I'm fresh," he said.

Oh God, she thought. His crazy behavior was some ghastly parody of teenaged dating, gleaned from old movies or comic books.

"And I will always respect you. I want to wait until we get married. But just tonight, just once, I want to see — " He trailed off, embarrassed.

Lowering his gaze, he began to fumble with the buttons on the front of her dress. There were five of them, and he took forever. She looked up at the sky, at the swirling fog above them, tears stinging her eyes.

When he had undone the five buttons, he used the tip of the knife to separate the two halves of the front of her dress. She wasn't wearing a bra. He looked at her breasts and then he said: "You shouldn't run around without any underwear like that. My mother says it's bad for women to do that. It ruins their figures."

He put the knife back in the pocket of his windbreaker.

"Please," sobbed Rebecca, "can we go home now?"

"All right," he said in a normal conversational tone.

She did her buttons up quickly and started down the beach running as fast as she could. He stayed right behind her. She wasn't trying to get away. She hadn't any more hope along those lines. She just wanted to end the ordeal as soon as possible.

Back in the car she broke down and began sobbing uncontrollably. He made no effort to comfort her, just looked over at her, puzzled. "I guess girls are more emotional than guys."

"Oh, please, take me home," she pleaded through her tears.

"There's just one thing, Rebecca. It's important to me." .

She rubbed her eyes, tilted her head back, sniffed, and tried to regain her composure. "What?" she demanded, hoarsely.

"I want you to tell me you love me. You do, you know."

"Oh, Benjamin, please. No more. Take me back. I can't take any more."

Once again the knife appeared before her, like some sort of talisman. This time he lowered it very delicately against her throat.

"I hate it when you make me use this," he said with a pout. "Now say it."

Choking, her eyes closed, her whole body trembling, she repeated after him: "I love you, Benjamin. I really love you."

4

Philip had wanted to comfort her throughout the story. He'd made soothing noises and approached her, but she shook her head and held up her hand to indicate she wanted to finish. Now that it was told up to the point where Benjamin Knapp had made her tell him she loved him, Rebecca stopped.

"And that," she said matter-of-factly, "was the first I ever had to do with Benjamin."

She expected Philip to take her in his arms. Intead, he sipped his coffee slowly, his brow furrowed. "So he just took you back to campus?"

"That's right."

"My God, Rebecca, the way you told it I thought he was going to rape you."

"That's what I thought at the time." She wanted Philip to know what it had been like.

"Well it's still a horrible story," he conceded.

"I could have lived with it, if that had been the end," said Rebecca.

49

"What do you mean?"

"Well, there was the trial. I foolishly had him prosecuted for assault. Pointing a knife at someone is assault, you know."

"What happened?"

Rebecca laughed bitterly. "The Knapps hired some expensive lawyers. They found witnesses at the party who said I was drinking. They had it brought out at the trial that I wasn't wearing a bra. They had private investigators try to prove I wasn't a virgin. Actually, at the time, I was. Anyway, when it was all over, the judge said what had happened was essentially a date that got out of hand. He told me it was up to the girl to keep things under control."

Philip looked horrified. She was glad. She had wanted him to be. He had passed another small test.

"But, Rebecca," he said, "what I don't understand is why this guy is sending me a telegram. The incident you're talking about is fifteen years ago."

Rebecca sighed. "That's right. That's the weird part. I've never been rid of him. He still thinks we're in love and meant to be together. He's spent years finding my unlisted phone numbers, harassing me and my boyfriends."

Philip rose and put his coffee cup down on the table. "My God, Rebecca, why didn't you tell me about him?"

She rubbed her forehead. "I thought it had stopped. I hadn't heard from Benjamin for a couple of years. I thought he'd finally been put away, or maybe he'd died, or even that he'd forgotten about me. I wanted to believe that."

Philip looked angry. "Don't you think I had a right to know? If this clown is going to barge in and . . . my God, Rebecca, do you think he's dangerous?"

She looked up at him. "I certainly thought so that first night," she said tartly. "Since then, I've done a little research on the syndrome."

"Syndrome?"

"It's called erotomania. Benjamin is an erotomaniac. It's only been named recently, but it's been around for years. Wait here."

She slid off the stool in the kitchen and went into her study. In an unmarked folder at the back of the bottom drawer of the filing cabinet was a pile of yellowed newspaper clippings. She brought them to the kitchen and handed them to Philip.

She knew them all practically by heart. Each described the murder of a woman. None had known her assailant well. But the men who had killed these women had spent months or years tracking them, trying to court them, following them, writing to them. These men had all declared their undying love for the women, and they had vowed that if they couldn't have them, no one would.

One of the killers met his victim at a charity dance. They danced twice, and he spent the next three years harassing her. He showered her with poems and letters, called her several times a day. The more she rebuffed him, the angrier he became. Soon, the letters were threatening. When she moved to another city, he followed her and stabbed her as she waited for a bus.

Another killer worked in the same building as the woman with whom he became obsessed. He kept asking her out, finally threatening her. She changed jobs and he took to parking outside her house for hours on end. He telephoned her daily and followed her when she went out with other men. She tried to get the police involved, but they laughed at her. "No law against being in love," one officer was quoted as saying when she went to file a complaint. Her tormentor shot her on the front porch as she went out to get the morning paper.

A third case involved a man who took the object of his twisted affection hostage for forty hours before killing her, then himself, with a shotgun blast. He'd first spotted her on a bicycle in a city park.

Rebecca fussed around the kitchen a little, wiping the counter, putting the coffee away, while Philip read the clippings. She knew she sounded hard when she talked about Benjamin. She didn't know how she could help that. But she still wished Philip would take her in his arms and tell her that she wouldn't be alone against Benjamin Knapp any more. Now there would be two of them. She folded the dish towel neatly and looked over at him as she hung it up.

"Jesus," said Philip. "And you think this Knapp guy could be one of these guys?"

She shrugged. "Who knows? He's been at it longer than any of them. The longest one in that collection is eight years. He's been following me around for almost twice that time."

"I can't believe you're engaged to me and you never told me about this." He sounded stern.

"I thought it was over." But had she really? Did she ever think it would be over?

Philip turned away from her. He seemed to be addressing the fridge. "I thought you were perfect. The perfect woman. Kind, funny, gorgeous, smart. A great career. Fun."

"Like someone in an ad for an upscale product," she heard herself saying bitterly. "And now you see me as flawed."

53

"Well, my God, Rebecca, if this guy's dangerous — and it sounds like he might be — I mean we need to get some help on this thing."

"There is no help," said Rebecca. "I learned that long ago. It's like being haunted by a demon, an unexorcisable demon."

"Come on," he said impatiently. "There must be some legal remedy."

She shrugged again. She felt like an old hand at this, a jaded old hand. No one else could possibly understand what it had been like to spend one's entire adult life stalked by Benjamin Knapp.

"I've been able to get injunctions once in a while. He usually pays attention to them. He has to stay twenty feet away and he can't call me on the phone. Of course, it's only a piece of paper. It can't really stop him. And it's only good here in California."

She thought grimly of her last year of graduate school in New York. Benjamin had followed her there and made her life hell. It was amazing she'd ever finished her dissertation.

"Well he's obviously nuts," said Philip impatiently. "He should be locked up somewhere."

"He's not a danger to himself or others. That's the way the state sees it. He has a good job. He keeps himself clean, pays his taxes. As far as I know, he's never even had a parking ticket. Outwardly, he's completely sane except that he thinks he's supposed to be married to me, and that I really love him. I just won't admit it."

"What about his parents?" said Philip helplessly. "Can't they do something?"

"Ha!" Rebecca knew she was sounding hard again. "His father's a retired general. He's embarrassed by Benjamin, but he's never cared for me. Thinks I drove his boy crazy. After that assault charge, the old guy whisked Benjamin out of Stanford and got him into the service. That allowed me to get through my undergraduate years without too much trouble, except the letters, of course. And then, whenever he was on leave he'd come and hang around outside wherever I was living. Later, Benjamin's father gave up on him completely."

She sighed. "His mother's different. She's bought into it. She sends me cards on my birthday and Christmas, hoping Benjamin and I will patch things up."

Philip looked at her intently. "Rebecca, I can't believe this. You're standing here talking about this like it's no big deal. And then you show me these!" He waved the clippings at her. "I don't understand you at all. I thought I knew you!"

"What was I supposed to do?" she said, becoming agitated. "I couldn't have spent my whole life in fear. I haven't had any choice. There's no point dwelling on what might happen. I've just had to live with it."

"I can't believe you didn't tell me."

She turned away from him. "I know, Philip. I wanted to. It's just that we were so happy. And Benjamin, well, he's an ugly part of my life. I didn't want to burden you with it."

"I suppose I would have found out after we were married," he said with a shudder.

"What's that supposed to mean?" she said. She had seen revulsion in that shudder. It was as if she had some horrible disease and he didn't want to become contaminated.

"Just what it says," he replied coldly. "I think it would have been decent if you'd warned me that I'm going to have to spend the rest of my life looking over my shoulder."

"I didn't think you'd be afraid," she said in a small, startled voice. "It never occurred to me."

"It's not that," he said hastily. "It's mostly that you didn't trust me enough to tell me."

"You're right," she said. "It sounds like a cliché, I know, but I'm afraid to trust. I suppose a shrink would say it was because of Benjamin."

"You didn't see a shrink to help you cope?" he said.

She shook her head. "I went once. He wanted me to talk about it until I wasn't frightened or angry. That's impossible. There's no way I can talk my way out of it. I've been marked, somehow, by Benjamin Knapp, and there's nothing I can do about it except learn to live with it."

"And you thought I could do that too. Except you didn't bother to tell me about it." Philip shook his head. "It's a damned shame. I guess none of it's been your fault, really. Your only crime was looking good."

She glanced at the clock on the stove. "It's late. Let's just forget about this for now, okay? We can talk about it in the morning." She went over to him, put her arms around his neck.

He kissed her lightly.

"Let's just go to bed," she said.

"I've got an early meeting," he said. "I think I'll go back to my place tonight. It's been a long night." With a smile and his easy charm, he added, "I won't get any sleep if I stay here. Not with you looking as gorgeous as you do."

She let go of him and tilted her face toward his with an appraising look. She tried to gauge his feelings and came up empty.

Later, after he left, she sat for a long time at her dressing table. Finally, she twisted off her emerald engagement ring and flung it carelessly on the table top. It came off easily. The dress, with all those buttons up the back, was much harder.

5

"Well, what do you think?"

Rebecca was in the office of her friend and lawyer, Angela Casaretti. Angela sat at her desk, tucking a wild mane of curly dark hair behind her ear and reading over the telegram Benjamin had sent Philip.

"I think we can do something," she said. "We can get a restraining order, probably. We can get a judge to tell him he can't communicate with Philip." She looked up at Rebecca. "I'm sorry," she said simply. "God, Rebecca, I wish I could have done something about this guy years ago. But the remedies aren't there."

"I don't want him bothering Philip," Rebecca said. "It's different for me. I'm almost used to it. It's like having diabetes or epilepsy or something. You learn to live with it."

"Benjamin Knapp is a disease, all right," said Angela with a shudder. Then she sighed. "I'll do this for you," she said, "but I have to advise you that it isn't the total solution. We can't predict what Benjamin's going to do next. We've been around and around with this guy long enough to know that, haven't we?"

"About fifteen years," said Rebecca.

"Oh my God, has it really been that long?" Angela had been a pre-law student during Benjamin Knapp's assault trial when they were all undergraduates at Stanford. "I'd have thought he would have backed off when he heard you were engaged. How did he find that out, by the way?"

"There was an item in Herb Caen's column," said Rebecca. "Some of Philip's friends planted it, I guess. It mentioned his firm."

"Just what you needed," said Angela. "Didn't he know about Benjamin?"

"I never told him," said Rebecca, looking away.

Angela sighed. "We'll see what we can do. I'll need Philip to sign some of the papers, of course. I take it he knows you're doing this? Trying to restrain Benjamin?"

Rebecca squirmed a little. "I've tried to keep it as low key as possible," she said. "Poor Philip seemed so agitated when he found out about Benjamin. I don't want to make a big deal of it. I just want to do what I can to keep Benjamin off his back." She leaned forward intently. "Angela," she said, "I never thought

I'd be as happy as I am now. I don't want that screwed up. It would be too much to take — first of all, to think I could never be so happy, then to find I could only to have it all taken away from me again. I can't give up on happiness without a fight."

Angela's heavy, dark brows rose. "A fight? What are you talking about? Do you think Benjamin could scare Philip off?"

"Of course not," said Rebecca. "It's just that he was so surprised I'd never told him about it. I think it made him wonder how close we are."

"Listen," said Angela, "I've done enough divorces to know that complete intimacy isn't always a good idea. I don't care what those ladies' magazines say." She smiled and patted Rebecca's hand. "I'll see what I can do," she said. "If all else fails, we can sue that little Knapp bastard for alienation of affection. Might be interesting to see how that would fly nowadays. Believe me, I'd love to have something to nail him with."

She sat back up and assumed a less personal tone. "Okay, I need his address."

"I don't have it. I tried to get it from directory assistance, but I can't find him."

"There's a detective we use a lot, one flight down in this building. Michael Caruso. Nice guy. He can probably find the guy for you in a

61

day. Want go to that route?"

"Sure."

"Okay." She checked her watch. "I'm going to be tied up in court all afternoon. If you really want to get rolling on this, why don't you stop by his office on your way out and see if he can see you? He isn't that busy. I bet he'll squeeze you in."

Rebecca didn't like Michael Caruso's office. Too bland and slick. A beige lobby with leather sofa and glass coffee table, the inevitable ficus tree shedding its leaves in the corner. An over made-up receptionist, clacking away on an electronic keyboard.

And she didn't like his manner. Too smooth. She sat on the sofa in the lobby waiting for her appointment and watched as Caruso emerged from behind a blond wood door. He was dark, in his mid-thirties, carefully dressed in white shirt and blue suit. He nodded at her curtly as he escorted a woman, presumably a distraught client, to the elevator. In late middle age with her hair dyed an impossible shade, she was bent forward over the handkerchief clutched in her hand. Caruso's hand was on her elbow, and his dark, sleek head was tilted toward her ear. He seemed to be murmuring soothingly.

Rebecca imagined that a great deal of his

business depended on comforting clients who had been hurt by someone they loved, hurt by someone who probably didn't deserve to be loved. Unfaithful husbands and wives. Half-grown children who drifted away. She sighed. It all seemed so depressing. Were there any happy families anymore? Was it colossal arrogance to think she could be part of one?

A moment later, Caruso returned to the lobby, and gave Rebecca a pleasant, reassuring smile. He had nice teeth. Rebecca didn't like men who looked so confident, but it didn't really matter whether she liked him or not. All she had to do was get him to do a simple job for her.

He led her into a small inner office, sat her down, looked bright and attentive. "Tell me why you came to see me," he said.

"I need to find someone. His name is Benjamin Knapp."

He nodded solemnly. Rebecca suddenly felt irritated. Most of his clients probably lived messy lives. Why else would they be consulting a private detective? There was nothing wrong with her life — at least not of her own making. But he probably thought she was another hysteric whose life had become a shambles — like the pathetic woman he'd led to the elevator.

"It's a legal matter," she said simply. "I

want him served, and I need to find him first."

"You want me to serve him too? I'd be glad to do that."

Rebecca thought for a second. She'd leave it up to her lawyer. "That won't be necessary," she said. "Just get me his address, will you?"

"Does this guy owe you money?" asked Caruso.

"No," said Rebecca a little coldly. "He doesn't."

"Usually, that's it," said Caruso. "And when that's the case, a lot of people are usually looking for the individual."

"He doesn't owe me money," said Rebecca.

"A personal matter then?" said Caruso.

"I suppose so," she said, almost shuddering. Through his own madness, Benjamin had become a part of her life. A personal matter. God, she hated him. Well, this time, she was going to do whatever it took to get him out of her life completely. She realized that she was gripping the desk in front of her. She looked down at her hands, the knuckles standing out whitely. Then she intercepted Caruso's glance. He was staring down at her knuckles too.

"Listen," said Caruso, "it's none of my business. I just want to tell you that sometimes I've found people and I wish I hadn't. Do you know what I mean? Are you sure you want me to find this man for you?"

"Of course I'm sure," she snapped.

He threw up his hands, held them in the air, palms facing her. "Okay. just thought I'd check. Sometimes it's better to forget about these guys." He smiled. "You're a smart, pretty lady — " he punctuated this with a smile and an appraising flicker of his eyes down from her face and back up again that she found offensive. "I'd hate to see you make yourself unhappy."

"It's Benjamin Knapp who's made me unhappy," she said angrily. Apparently he thought she was carryng some sort of a torch for Benjamin and was trying to tell her in his crude way that she was marketable enough to find someone else. "It's very simple. I'm hiring you to do a job. You don't need to bother about my motivation. Or flatter me either." She stared at Caruso, who was looking at her now with heavy-lidded, solemn brown eyes. He seemed to be feeling sorry for her, but she decided it was simply a bedside manner he'd developed to deal with his hysterical clients.

There was something so undignified, she thought, about sitting here with a stranger, at the edge of a nervous collapse, and looking up to see mock pity. It was just one of hundreds of small indignities Benjamin Knapp had inflicted on her over the years. The burden of all those moments suddenly seemed to overwhelm her, and she slumped in her chair a little; tears of anger springing to her eyes. "Well," she said irritably, "will you find him for me?"

"Sure," said Michael Caruso. He pushed a box of Kleenex toward her, and she ignored it, straightening in her chair and trying to blink back her tears. "Tell me his full name. Where he works if you know it. Known associates."

She gave him the information, avoiding his eyes. "His name is Benjamin James Knapp. I don't know where he works, but I would like to know. He's around here somewhere in the Bay Area, and his last job was working with computers. He's very close to his mother. I have her address here. She lives down on the Peninsula."

Although Caruso's tone was now strictly businesslike, she gazed above him at a Japanese print on the wall. She wanted to make sure she didn't cry, or let the tears in the corners of her eyes spill onto her cheeks. She'd hated the way he'd pushed that box of Kleenex at her. Men, she reflected, probably liked seeing women cry. It made them feel superior and in control. Isn't that what they all wanted? Isn't that what Benjamin Knapp wanted?

After she left, Caruso sighed and tipped back in his chair. There were a lot of angry women in the world, he reflected, and he'd just met another one. He toyed briefly with the idea of turning down all domestic cases, which was exactly how he classified this one. Business was picking up. He was getting enough corporate clients to get a little picky and forget about some of this messy personal stuff.

Caruso decided he'd rather identify a ring of crooked employees stealing merchandise out of a warehouse, or figure which cashier was skimming the cash receipts at a restaurant than deal with the angry or the heartbroken.

He sighed and reached for the telephone. He made two phone calls to what he euphemistically referred to as "confidential sources" — low-level employees of the phone company who had access to computer records and provided phone numbers and addresses at a hundred bucks a pop. Benjamin James Knapp's place of employment came from phone company credit records. That cost a little more. Knapp worked at a fairly large insurance company in Alameda across the bay. Caruso knew he had the right Benjamin Knapp, because the records showed he'd used his mother as a credit reference years ago when he got his first phone. That address matched the address the Kendall woman had given him.

All in all, it was a pretty easy piece of work. All he had to do now was mark up his expenses — he usually just doubled what the crooked employees charged him — and bill for his time. This time it was an hour, because he never billed in smaller increments.

He wondered what the real story was with Rebecca Kendall. After their meeting, she'd stormed out of his office so quickly that Gail, the receptionist, who never let anyone get out of the waiting area without paying a hefty deposit, wasn't able to stop her. Caruso had been in business long enough to sense who'd skip, and this woman didn't fit the profile. But there was something out of the ordinary about her.

Usually, women who were looking for the men who'd vanished from their lives wanted to talk about it. Usually, there was — mixed with the anger and grief — some residual affection for the guys, some sexual longing, some pathetic conviction that it could all be put back together. All he'd seen from Rebecca Kendall was rage. She wasn't stupid. The woman was a college professor. Maybe she was crazy. He decided to instruct Gail to call the woman and get her to come in person to pick up the information, as well as drop off a check.

It wasn't just the money, he realized. It was this nagging feeling that he didn't know what it was Rebecca Kendall was up to. He felt a lack of control when he wasn't sure of the emotions that drove his clients. He hated that feeling, so he looked forward to seeing Rebecca Kendall again, and taking one more shot at figuring out what kind of a beef she had with Benjamin Knapp.

A day later, Rebecca Kendall was back in his inner office, glaring at him. Caruso didn't know what her connection was with this Benjamin character, but he was beginning to feel sorry for the guy. Rebecca Kendall was one tough, mean woman. Good-looking, too, and probably aware of it, even though she had a cold, stiff personality, stripped of any female flirtatiousness. As he handed the folder over to her, he almost felt as if he were violating some sense of solidarity with a fellow male.

"Here's what you were looking for," he said simply. Then, because she didn't smile or say thank you, and because she seemed to have no sense of humor and to take herself too damn seriously, and because she'd rejected his standard offer of sympathy and understanding when he'd first taken the assignment, and because he still didn't know where she was coming from, he gave her a sideways little smile and said, "Hope you'll go easy on the guy when you get hold of him." It was insolent and unprofessional, but that was the whole point of being a private investigator instead of a cop on the public payroll. You didn't have to be polite.

Rebecca Kendall looked up at him and said with mock sweetness: "I don't owe you any explanation. But I can honestly say I wish I could kill him. Any jury in the world would understand." She gave him a strained, artificial smile. "All right?"

His face remained impassive, but he flung down the pen he happened to be holding with a gesture that revealed his annoyance. "Gail will have your bill for you on your way out," he said.

After she left, he started to worry.

6

She was trembling when she left Caruso's office. She had lost emotional control. Maybe because she'd begun to cry the first time she'd been in his office, she'd tried too hard to keep herself in check this time. She realized she'd snapped at him. She was ashamed of herself.

Waiting in front of the elevator, she took a deep breath and blinked hard, as if warning herself not to cry. It wasn't that she cared what Caruso thought. Rather, it was the fact that every time Benjamin managed to make her behave in a way contrary to her basic nature, she felt devastated. She sometimes wondered what kind of a woman she would have become if she had never met Benjamin Knapp, but she didn't like to think about that for too long. In any case, now that Philip was in her life, she felt as if Benjamin, like the bad fairy at Sleeping Beauty's christening, was about to have his spell broken.

She smiled at the thought of Philip. She checked her watch. She'd call him now and see if he could meet her for lunch. That would cheer her up. But first, she'd deliver the information Caruso had gathered to Angela's office upstairs.

A few days later, Caruso found himself thinking about Rebecca Kendall. He had plenty of time to think. He was looking for a skip — and he'd been parked for hours in front of a particularly depressing bar in Oakland. If his information was correct, his guy would show up here sooner or later. Caruso had spent some time inside the bar, and he'd established that the guy was a regular, but after a few watery Scotches and a lot of stupid conversation, he'd decided he'd be happier sitting in the car.

By two A.M., when the place closed, his guy still hadn't showed up. Caruso sighed, put the car in gear, and promised himself a decent drink when he got home. But first, just because he'd been thinking about Benjamin Knapp and his weird client, Rebecca Kendall, he thought he'd cruise by the address he'd found for her. It was nearby, in the hills above Oakland.

You could tell a lot about a person just cruising by the house. Caruso figured this Knapp character was probably married. That would fit. There'd be a couple of tricycles on the front lawn, maybe a cocker spaniel. A station wagon for the wife and something sportier for Benjamin. After all, he was a sporty kind of guy.

That might help Caruso understand why Rebecca Kendall was so damned mad at this Knapp character. Caruso had met dozens of single females — attractive, intelligent, and just plain foolish. Why were they always so amazed to learn that their lovers, ardent but invariably pressed for time, were married with wives and kids stashed in the suburbs? It took the women even longer to realize the guys never had any intentions of leaving their families.

He hoped that was the scenario here. Then he'd know for certain what the deal was with Rebecca Kendall and he could forget all about her.

He got a funny feeling early on, though. The street was all wrong. It wasn't middle-class enough. You'd expect someone with enough going for him to seduce a good-looking educated woman like the Kendall woman, to come from somewhere a little classier. You never knew, though. Some of these career women pushing forty could get pretty desperate these days.

But then, the house was wrong too. It was secluded, a little square box tucked at the end of a cul-de-sac. It wasn't big enough for a family. And it was too neat to be anything but the home of a fussy bachelor. There was an unimaginative landscaping scheme, featuring a row of marigolds and a green, well-tended square of lawn. There was even a white picket fence. The place looked like a little old lady lived there. ⁓

Caruso prepared to turn around at the end of the road, and gave the place one last glance. Then he stopped the car. There was something definitely odd about the place. He got the same fluttery feeling of trouble he used to get when he was back on a beat. The door to the prim little house was wide open. The front door. At two-thirty in the morning.

Caruso parked the car, set the brake, took a deep breath, and decided to check it out. If there'd been a vehicle out front, he would have called it as a burglary in progress.

He didn't know what to expect, but by the time he reached the porch, he thought he knew. Blood has an unmistakable smell, and it hit him as soon as he stood on the porch. Judging by the collection of flies buzzing around the living room, the door had been open and the blood luring them in there for some time.

The lights were out in the tiny living room, but there was a glow coming from the kitchen. Caruso, wary but still curious, went in. There

74

was a bloody towel in the sink, smears of blood on the worn linoleum, a trail of more smears leading to a back bedroom. Caruso knew he should get out now and call the cops, but he kept going. He went into the bedroom and saw the bed, sheets half off, striped mattress ticking exposed. The mattress was saturated with blood, and it still looked wet. The smell of it was overpowering. More rusty-looking spots of blood stained the wall above the bed, and there were signs of a struggle — an overturned bedside table, a lamp on its side on the floor, still lit, sending out light at a crazy angle, throwing a beam into a corner of the ceiling and casting a sickly ambient light on everything else.

It was possible, he thought, trying not to gag, that these weren't the signs of a struggle. They might be signs of panic after committing a brutal act. Like the pathetic towel in the sink — as if anyone could clean up such a mess.

Caruso checked the bathroom and the second bedroom, set up like an office with a computer and a neat stack of papers on a desk, for the body. There wasn't one. But something pretty major had happened here, there was no doubt about it.

Without touching anything, he tried to get a feeling for the person who lived here. It looked spartan and temporary. There were no pictures on the wall, and just a few books, mostly about computers, although there were also some spy novels. A rack held a small collection of magazines — three devoted to computers and two about bodybuilding. A four-day-old *Oakland Tribune* was neatly folded there too.

There was some mail on the carpet in front of the slot in the front door — a phone bill, a circular from Sears, and a Pacific Gas and Electric bill. They were all addressed to Benjamin Knapp.

Caruso went to the phone and, ever mindful of preserving the scene, picked up the receiver with a handkerchief. Then he telephoned the police.

The dispatcher told him to leave the house and wait for the police in his car. He didn't bother to tell her that he'd been a police officer himself, and that he might just as well stay on the premises. Not that there was anything to do. The scene was secure. But Caruso felt like a cop on duty — like something had happened on his beat. He was afraid it was because of Rebecca Kendall, because he'd given her this address.

7

A foghorn sounded. Rebecca tossed a little in her sleep, twisted around, and fell against Philip's sleeping form. Smiling slightly, she settled her head against his shoulder and drifted back to sleep.

Then the bell rang, a shrill blast that made her sit nearly straight up. She glanced around and saw the pale gleam of dawn between the louvers in the blinds at the window.

The bell rang again, and this time she slid out of bed, grabbed a bathrobe, and went over to the intercom that connected her apartment with the street below. "Who is it?" she demanded sharply, thinking that perhaps it would have been better if Philip had answered. After all, this was a weird time of the morning to be ringing her doorbell. She even wondered if it could be Benjamin.

"Police," came the reply. "Are you Rebecca Kendall?"

"Yes," she said, puzzled. "Is everything all

right?" She strained to hear through the static of the machine.

"Can we come up and talk to you?"

"All right, I guess," she said uncertainly, buzzing them into the building.

With the chain still on the door she examined the heavy police badge through the small space it allowed, then opened the door, and was surprised to see four men standing there. One of them, to her astonishment, was Michael Caruso.

"I guess you know Mr. Caruso," said the detective who'd shown her his badge. "I'm Lieutenant Caldwell from the San Francisco Police. These two gentlemen are from across the Bay. They believe a crime was committed in Oakland last night, and they'd like to ask you a few questions. All right?"

"What crime?" She drew the sash of her bathrobe tighter around her and put a hand self-consciously to her hair, pushing it away from her face. "I'm sorry, but I'm confused."

"We believe a murder was committed recently," began one of the Oakland detectives. "At the home of Benjamin Knapp. In fact, we have reason to suspect Mr. Knapp has been murdered."

"Benjamin? Dead?" Her eyes widened, her mouth curved into a smile, tears came into her eyes. "Thank God," she said.

The men exchanged glances.

"I know it sounds harsh, but Benjamin Knapp has made my life hell for so long. Please come in. Do you want coffee or something?"

They all shook their heads. Rebecca led them into the living room in a slight daze.

"So you did know Benjamin Knapp," Caldwell said.

"I guess so," she said, vaguely indicating chairs and the sofa. "I mean, I never sought out his company. Benjamin has been stalking me for years. It's a rather bizarre story, I'm afraid."

"Mr. Caruso says you were trying to find him," the man continued. She glanced over at Caruso. He looked back, his gaze steady, dark-eyed, and unsmiling.

"Oh," she said, catching on at last. "He brought you here. He thought . . . "

Caruso spoke up. "I felt I had to tell the police that you had made threatening remarks about Mr. Knapp," he said.

"You did? Why, that's ridiculous!" She looked angry, but a second later she had pulled herself together. "Naturally, you had to do what you thought best," she said. "But how did you know that Benjamin . . . "

"Mr. Caruso came on the scene." The Oakland detective spoke up. "He called us. I must impress on you, Miss Kendall, that we don't know that Benjamin Knapp was murdered. We are, however, operating on that assumption until we learn differently and pending the outcome of certain lab tests."

"I found a lot of blood," said Caruso simply. "A lot of blood and signs of a struggle."

"So he could be alive," said Rebecca. "Or just wounded."

"We don't think so," said the policeman. "No one could have lost that much blood and lived. That's what the doctor says."

She turned away. "I see."

Just then, Philip came into the room. He was wearing his wine-colored wool bathrobe, and his hair was tousled. He brushed it with his fingers when he saw the men. "What's going on, Rebecca?"

"These are policemen. This is my fiancé, Philip Patterson. They've come to tell me they think Benjamin Knapp has been murdered."

"That's terrible," said Philip. Rebecca assumed Philip was just making a conventional show of shock, but she was ashamed at her own reaction a moment earlier. What must the police think of her?

"Miss Kendall didn't think so," said Caruso.

"This is Michael Caruso," explained Rebecca. "He's a private investigator. I hired him to find Benjamin, so I could serve him with papers."

"Why?" said Philip, frowning in confusion. "What's going on, Rebecca?"

"I hadn't talked to you about it yet," she said, trying to keep her voice steady. Panic began to rise in her. She felt out of control. "I wanted to surprise you." It sounded absurd, as if she were buying him a treat. "I was getting a restraining order, making sure Benjamin didn't harass you anymore. After that telegram."

"Oh, that wasn't necessary," said Philip. He looked embarrassed that he hadn't known about her plans. "You should have talked to me about it." He went over to her and put a proprietary arm around her shoulder.

She sat down heavily on the sofa, and Philip sat next to her. She felt light-headed. The police were talking now, asking her about Benjamin, but she couldn't concentrate on their questions. Benjamin was dead and she felt like laughing out loud.

"Mind if we take a look around?" the Oakland detective was asking now.

"That's ridiculous," said Philip. "Have you got a warrant?"

"No, but we can go get one and come right back," said the detective evenly.

She was irritated that Philip seemed to be

speaking for her. "Of course they can look around," she said. "The sooner they realize how ridiculous this whole thing is, the better. Then they'll leave us alone."

"Rebecca," said Philip brusquely, "don't you think you'd better call your lawyer?"

"Angela? Why?"

"Do me a favor," said Philip. "Talk to Angela. I'll call her."

"Don't be silly," said Rebecca. "I haven't got anything to hide. I can't imagine why they're here at all, except Mr. Caruso told the police I was looking for Benjamin and threatened him." She tried to speak evenly, calmly.

"Well that's a hell of a note," snapped Philip at Caruso. "What about client confidentiality? That's not too professional, is it?"

Caruso leaned toward Philip belligerently but kept his voice steady. "I'm not an attorney and I'm not a priest. I'll shut up about a client's indiscretions as a professional courtesy, but that isn't the client's right. I won't shut up about murder. That kind of loyalty's not for sale. Miss Kendall will just have to tell her story to the police. I came along to make a simple identification. Now that I've done that, I'll be going."

Rebecca rose instinctively, as if to show him out. Why was she so polite? This man had just brought the police to her door.

"Don't bother to see me out," he said, turning from her and heading into the hall. Watching his back, she felt his repugnance and realized he wanted to get out of her apartment as soon as he could. It was as if the hideous qualities of Benjamin Knapp had contaminated her.

Down on the street, Caruso put his hands in his pockets and decided to walk the twenty blocks or so home. His car was still over in Oakland. He'd sleep, shower, and shave, then go into the office and have Gail drive him over to pick it up. He'd been up all night, hanging out with the cops, watching them pick through the crime scene. He'd told them about Rebecca Kendall, then tagged along to her apartment.

But after all that, Caruso had more questions than answers. In his experience, most human behavior fit into rather shabby and predictable patterns. Nothing about this deal fit at all. The last thing he'd expected was that good-looking fiancé in a monogrammed bathrobe. He'd thought she was pining away for this Knapp character.

All Caruso knew for sure was that when Rebecca Kendall was told Benjamin Knapp might be dead, her expression had softened, making her look ten years younger.

8

"But you did hate him, didn't you?" One of the policemen leaned back and smiled at her across the table.

"Yes, but what does that have to do with . . ."

Angela interrupted. "Either arrest her or let her go now," she said evenly.

"It's all right," said Rebecca. "I didn't do it. I didn't do anything."

"That's not the point," said Angela, standing and pulling her handbag strap over her shoulder. "Come on, Rebecca." They were sitting in a small glassed-in conference room at police headquarters in downtown Oakland.

"But they can't arrest me," said Rebecca "They don't even have a body." She was tired. She'd been here almost an hour and a half, patiently answering all their questions, certain that if they would just listen to her they'd understand that she couldn't possibly know anything about Benjamin Knapp's disappearance, or why his mattress was soaked with blood.

Just about ten minutes ago, Angela had arrived, bustling into the room, interrupting the almost languid exchange of questions and answers between Rebecca and her interrogators. At the sight of Angela, her long cardigan flapping, arms waving, her familiar voice breaking in at its rapid clip, Rebecca realized that until now, there had been something rather surreal about her session with the police. She'd come voluntarily, wanting to make it clear to them she wasn't involved, but they seemed not to understand. They were asking the same questions over and over, asking her why she hated Benjamin, telling her that maybe it was all right for someone to have murdered him, waiting for her to agree.

"Are you under the impression that we can't indict you without finding a body?" asked the detective.

"Don't answer that," Angela snapped to Rebecca. "I'm your attorney, and I'm advising you right now to go home. They can't grill you forever about this."

She took Rebecca's arm to lead her from the room. "For God's sake, Rebecca," she said, after they were out of earshot and had nodded vaguely at the policeman's admonition to stay in the Bay Area and be available for more questioning. "Why didn't you call me right away? If Philip hadn't alerted me, I suppose you would have spent all day chatting with those cops. You didn't have to come down here and be questioned.

"And," she added, frowning, "you certainly didn't need to let them cart all that stuff away from your house."

"I don't know why they took anything," said Rebecca. "There's nothing there that could possibly — "

"That's not what those detectives are thinking. Not if their questions are any indication. What in God's name is going on, Rebecca? Philip says they took stuff from your car. Were they just on a fishing expedition or what? Did they have a warrant?"

Rebecca sighed. "I told them they could look around. I don't understand, Angela. I don't know what's going on."

"And how in hell did they come to your apartment in the first place?" continued Angela.

"Michael Caruso."

"What? *My* Michael Caruso? The Italian stallion on the fourth floor? What did he have to do with it?"

"He told them I'd threatened Benjamin, and that I'd been trying to find his address."

"Well that's not enough for a murder indictment," said Angela heatedly. "My God, Rebecca, what have you got yourself into?"

Out in the hall, Rebecca, who'd been pale but controlled while she was being questioned, suddenly felt weak. "Angela, I don't think I can make it," she said. "I've got to sit down for a minute."

Angela guided her to a sorrowful-looking sofa in the outer lobby. Rebecca's knees buckled under her and she sat down heavily.

"Angela, they think I did it. I can't believe it, but they think I did it. It just struck me."

"You should have called me when they came to your apartment in the first place. Philip tells me that you came with them to make a voluntary statement." Angela sighed. "Listen, Rebecca, I want you to get hold of yourself. Whatever's happened, now's not the time to fall apart. You need a good lawyer."

"Yes, you're right. That's why I'm so glad you're here," said Rebecca, touching Angela's arm. "I'm so confused."

"Not me," said Angela impatiently. "You need a good criminal lawyer. The best. I'm going to try and get Trevor Keegan for you."

"What?" Rebeccca's head seemed to clear immediately. "Angela, you think I'm in real trouble, don't you?"

Angela rolled her eyes in exasperation. "We're talking about a murder indictment," she said. "I don't know what they've got on you, but I know that the time for you to get good representation is before they hand down an indictment."

"But they don't even have a body."

"For some reason," said Angela, "a lot of people think you can't prosecute a murder where there's no body. It's not true."

Rebecca rose. "Let's go, Angela I'm so tired all of a sudden."

"Maybe everything will be all right," said Angela. "I'm not saying they'll indict you. I just want you to be prepared for the worst."

"But I didn't kill him," said Rebecca simply.

"That's not the point. The point is, you've got to look out for your own best interests right now. Let me call Keegan."

"You don't think I killed him, do you?" said Rebecca, her eyes widening.

"What I think isn't important. It's what a grand jury might think." They were at the elevator doors now. Angela jabbed the button impatiently and spoke in an urgent whisper. "Rebecca, I want you to concentrate. I know this has all been a terrible shock and you've been through a lot. You must feel terrible right now. But I want you to keep a level head. I want you to see Keegan, no matter how confused and awful you feel right now."

"But I don't feel awful, Angela. No one seems to understand that. I don't feel awful at all. Don't you understand? Benjamin's dead."

The elevator arrived, full of people. Both women remained silent as it descended.

As soon as they were out on the street, Rebecca turned to Angela. "I guess you'd better go ahead and call Keegan," she said. "If you're not sure whether I did it or not, I guess I'm going to need someone like him."

Angela didn't respond the way Rebecca had wanted her to. She'd hoped Angela would say, "But of course you didn't do it. I know that." Instead she looked relieved and said, "I'll call him right away. This is just the kind of case he loves."

"What do you mean? What kind of case is that?"

"Trevor Keegan built a fabulous career on sensational criminal trials. If this case ever comes to trial, and you're the defendant, it'll be sensational, believe me. If that means you can be represented by Trevor Keegan, well then maybe that's your first lucky break in a long time."

A week later, the detectives who'd interrogated Rebecca Kendall met with a lawyer from the Alameda County District Attorney's Office. The two policemen crowded into his smallish office, leaning forward as he went through the manila file they had brought.

Carl Applegate was very fair, with red-gold hair and pale young skin. He had a hawkish profile and light blue eyes. Long-limbed, he sprawled in his chair as if it were too small for him and propped up his feet on the wastebasket. "It's all circumstantial," he said.

"So?" said the first detective. "Unfortunately, people aren't always obliging enough to kill each other in front of eyewitnesses."

Applegate frowned. "Well jeez, couldn't you at least find the body?"

The second detective sighed. "We're working on it. Could be anywhere. It's pretty clear the body was transported in her car."

"Anyway," said his companion, "the doctor says no one could have lost that much blood and lived."

"We know it's his blood?" persisted Applegate.

The first policeman shrugged. "O-positive. Pretty common, but we know that was his type. Can't get any closer without a sample that we know came from Benjamin Knapp." He laughed. "Look at it this way, counselor — if she didn't do this Knapp character, she did someone else, with his blood type. And carried the body around in her car. We can match the blood from her trunk and from the scene very precisely with these new methods the lab's got."

Carl Applegate set down the folder and swung his legs to the floor.

"Did she do it?" he said. "You guys have any doubt?"

"She did it all right," said the second policeman.

"Why?" said Applegate.

The man shrugged. "Why does anyone fly off the handle and kill someone? She and this guy had a history that goes way back. Bad blood. They've been in and out of court over the years. Some weird sex thing, as far as I can tell. Knapp's mother said the Kendall woman has been obsessed with her son for years."

Applegate looked out of the window for a moment. "I want to get more than that. I want to be able to paint a complete picture for the jury — and I'm betting this is a jury trial."

The second detective fidgeted a little in his chair. "What makes you say it'll be a jury trial?" he said.

Applegate turned and smiled. "I heard a rumor Rebecca Kendall's got Trevor Keegan lined up in case we get an indictment. He always goes for a jury.

"To nail her, I have to know everything about this woman. Everything that's happened since she first met Benjamin Knapp."

"To help you, I've got to know everything. Everything about you and Benjamin Knapp." Trevor Keegan and Rebecca Kendall sat on red plush furniture in a small room at his law office in a perfectly renovated Victorian. Taking a sip of coffee from a flowery cup, Rebecca looked around her. Red plush draperies were tied back with golden tassels, and the flocked wallpaper was red too.

He caught her glance. "Place looks like a whorehouse, doesn't it?" He smiled. "One of my ex-wives decorated it. Unspeakably vulgar. The decor, I mean, not my ex-wife, particularly." Keegan looked strangely gray and dull in the flamboyant surroundings. In his late fifties, he was of medium height with a florid complexion and thick gray hair. He had the dark brows and lashes and smoky blue eyes of the black Irish, and a craggy face. He had a belligerent way of holding his head back and his chin up, but fortunately for him, as it was a great asset for a trial lawyer, he had a suave and rich baritone voice.

Rebecca gave him a frosty little smile. "Benjamin Knapp," she said. "It's a long story, Mr. Keegan."

He held up his hand. "Wait a minute, wait a minute," he said. "Before you tell me, let me tell you how much money this is going to cost you. Thirty thousand dollars. Is this going to present a problem?"

Rebecca turned a little pale. "I'm not sure. How can anyone afford you?"

He shrugged. "They manage. Usually their families come through. Mom and Dad take out a second mortgage. Thirty thousand is cheap at the price, let me tell you. We're talking about first-degree murder." He smiled. "Of course, if we get it knocked down to manslaughter, the price stays the same."

"I'll see what I can do."

"Good." He raised his hand admonishingly. "The price is the same whatever the verdict is. Because that thirty thousand gets you the best defense money can buy. You'll get the money somehow. Everyone does."

Angela had told her she wouldn't like Trevor Keegan. "He's a real son of a bitch," she had said. "He doesn't give a damn about his clients, so don't expect him to hold your hand and act sympathetic. He only cares about winning, and he's won way more than his fair share."

"I'll see what I can do," said Rebecca. "I have some equity in my condominium. And I might be able to get my hands on my retirement money."

"You'll manage," he said airily. "Thirty thousand isn't that much these days. Now, tell me about Benjamin. I guess the most important thing for me to know, right at the outset, is the truth. Remember, I'm your lawyer. Anything you tell me goes with me to my grave. You're an intelligent woman — a university professor, for God's sake — so you'll understand it when I tell you that my ability to defend you increases proportionately with my grasp of the true facts of this case. Now, did you kill Benjamin Knapp?"

"No," said Rebecca. "I didn't."

Trevor Keegan leaned back in his wing chair and looked at her long and hard. He seemed to expect her to get flustered, to change her mind, to say yes. For one crazy moment, Rebecca even felt an urge to do just that, to lean toward this rumpled man in the gray silk suit, to burst into tears, to confess. "Yes, I killed him," she could say. "And I'm glad I did." In a way it would be easier. But it wasn't true.

"No, I didn't," she repeated with irritation in her voice.

"If you're telling the truth," replied Trevor Keegan after a long pause, "It's a real shame. Because I could get you off a hell of a lot easier if you had done it."

9

"I don't know why he wants to get together in a restaurant," said Rebecca to Philip, looking around the room quickly. Then, after meeting several honestly curious stares that turned into the well-bred furtive glances one would expect from this quiet, very expensive restaurant, she turned hastily back to him.

Philip gazed around. "I guess the old boy wants to be seen in a restaurant with his beautiful and notorious client and her handsome fiancé." He gave her a little smile, and because she appreciated his trying to cheer her up, she smiled back, but she felt sick. She'd felt sick for weeks, it seemed, a gnawing pain in her stomach, a tenseness that never went away. She'd been waking up regularly every morning at four A.M.. "Come on, Rebecca, everyone knows Trevor Keegan loves publicity. If he didn't, we wouldn't be eating here, of all places."

Rebecca glanced at him sideways. "The way you're looking around," she said, "you'd think you like the publicity too."

He turned to her sharply. "Are you kidding? This has been a ghastly nightmare from the very beginning — ever since I got that damn telegram." He kissed her just above the eyebrow, and she smiled, noticing from the corner of her eye that two women at another table had observed this kiss and were whispering about it.

The maître d' approached, with Trevor Keegan in his wake. Keegan, looking smaller than he did in his Victorian parlor of an office, smiled affably at everyone in the restaurant and beamed at Rebecca. He came forward, managed somehow to seize her by the shoulders and get her to her feet, gave her a heartfelt kiss on the cheek, which flustered her, then shook Philip's hand.

When the three of them had settled back around the table, Rebecca felt the room settle back down with them. It was clear they had become the center of attention. She felt herself blushing. Ever since her arrest and subsequent release on bail, Rebecca had been recognized and observed. She'd taken to wearing jeans and sweatshirts, and tying her hair back severely from her face, which seemed to make her harder to recognize. But today, especially with Trevor Keegan there, everyone was watching her.

"All right," said Keegan, as soon as the waiter had handed around menus and departed. "Let's set a few basic ground rules. I went over this with Rebecca, but I want Philip to hear it firsthand."

Philip looked attentive and businesslike. Rebecca watched him as Trevor Keegan leaned across the table and said firmly, "Mr. Patterson, from now on, I want you and Rebecca to go everywhere together. When the trial starts, I want you at the defense table every day. I want you to come into court with your fiancée clinging to your arm, and I want you to stand up tall and brave. If you hear anything in court that sounds bad for Rebecca, I want you to turn to her, smile, pat her hand. When you get in front of those TV cameras crouching in wait for you at the bottom of the courthouse steps, I want you to put your arm around her and sweep her past them like Sir Galahad. Think you can handle all that? You look the part, anyway."

Philip glanced over at Rebecca, as if asking her whether she wanted him to help her this way. She turned to Trevor Keegan. "Is all this necessary? I kind of resent your making me out to be a helpless little thing, leaning on a man."

Trevor Keegan signaled the waiter. "You're accused of a brutal crime and you want to get off. You'd better not look too tough. Helpless is better.

"You want to look like your own life was in good shape, and you had no reason to kill Benjamin Knapp, so you make sure the world knows you've got a handsome, protective fiancé.

"And remember one thing. You *are* helpless right now, and you do need a man. Me. If Philip here wasn't available, I'd have you leaning on me. But he's taller and better looking." Rebecca didn't know if Keegan was joking or not with this last sally. She managed a polite smile.

"If you think it'll help, I guess we'd better — " She turned questioningly to Philip. "It seems silly, I know, but — "

"But I may not be able to get away from work — " began Philip. "That is, I'm not sure what my boss — "

Trevor Keegan smiled and ordered a martini for himself. Rebecca ordered a sherry and Philip a glass of white wine. As soon as the waiter left, Keegan's smile vanished and he leaned toward Philip. "You're a stockbroker, right? Well, listen, if this trial goes the wrong way, your career might be in pretty bad shape. Who wants to take financial advice from a guy so dumb he doesn't know he's sleeping with a cold-blooded killer?" He leaned back and the smile reappeared. "Think about it. When you do, talk to your boss. Take a leave of absence."

"Well of course," said Philip. "I just meant it might be awkward."

"Rebecca and I need you," said Keegan. With an impatient little gesture, he added, "Maybe the kind of man who took care of his woman — who wanted to take care of her — is gone. In your generation, anyway. But the public wishes he weren't. So be that guy."

"Naturally I'll do whatever I can to help Rebecca," said Philip stiffly. "There's no question about that."

"Good, good," said Keegan. "Now there's one more thing I wanted to discuss with you, Mr. Patterson. I'm worried about Rebecca. She's been under a lot of strain lately. I've been trying to get her to see a psychiatrist. Dr. Greenberg's a great guy." He sipped his martini and looked across at Rebecca as if she were a naughty child. "She won't do it."

"I hate psychiatry," said Rebecca. "It's an inexact science." She repressed the urge to tell him not to speak of her in the third person in her presence.

"You're absolutely right," said Keegan. "What those guys say shouldn't be admissible in court. But it is. It might help us."

"But why should Rebecca see a shrink if she's innocent?" said Philip.

Rebecca ignored him. "You contradicted yourself," she said to Keegan. "Do you want me to see a psychiatrist because of the strain of the trial, or because you want me to plead insanity or something? What have you got in mind?"

"Why do you think I want you to see a psychiatrist?" said Keegan mildly, fixing his shiny blue eyes rather intently on her.

Her mouth twitched into an irritated half smile. "Angela told me you don't give a damn about your clients. You just care about winning."

Keegan laughed. "That's right. And I want you to see a shrink to see if we can't come up with a better plea. Not insanity, necessarily. Diminished capacity, maybe. Bring in all the stuff this Knapp character put you through. We could put together a real elegant defense for you if you'd cooperate."

"But I'm not guilty," Rebecca whispered. "You can't even talk like this. I made it clear. I'm not guilty."

"There are two kinds of guilty," said Keegan. "There's the kind of guilty with which the Almighty concerns himself. I leave that to him. Then there's a plea or verdict of guilty. That's my province. And my job is to keep you out of prison. I'm telling you I can do a better job defending you if

100

you'll let me do it my way."

"But you're asking me to plead guilty when I'm not," said Rebecca. "My God, it's outrageous." She gathered up her purse. "I'm leaving."

"I never said that," said Keegan smoothly. "I merely advised you that it might make some sense to talk to this psychiatrist. We may be able to come up with a better plea."

"But it would be a lie." She turned to Philip. "Are you coming with me?"

Keegan's hand shot out and wrapped itself around her wrist. "Don't leave this table," he said. "Don't you dare leave this table."

Philip said softly, "Rebecca, listen to him."

"You want me to plead guilty to a crime I didn't commit?" She tried to keep her voice low, but she couldn't hide her indignation.

"I want you to be free. I want us to be together."

Rebecca looked down at her wrist. Keegan's hand still held it firmly. "Of course we won't plead you guilty against your will," he said. "We can't do that. But goddamn it, that story of yours about this Knapp character is a real heartbreaker. I can do something with that. Give me something to work with and I can set you free." And with that, he lifted his hand from her wrist in a light, birdlike gesture.

10

The day before her trial began, Rebecca sat in Trevor Keegan's Victorian parlor. He sat opposite her, with his usual bland smile. "Now tomorrow in court, I want you to sit at the end of the defense table, close to the jury," he said. "I'll be on the other side of you. That way, you'll look exposed and more vulnerable. Philip will sit right behind you, and I want you to turn to him for reassurance now and then."

"Do I have to look so helpless?" she said.

"You sure do," he said. "Certainly too helpless to have murdered anyone. Now for God's sake, don't bring anything but a handbag. No legal pads or anything. I don't want you taking notes." His voice took on more emotion. "I hate it when clients do that. It looks like they don't trust me to handle the case by myself. The jury's got to see me in complete control. I've got to keep them with me from the beginning."

"I'm nervous about the jury," said Rebecca.

She abandoned her red plush sofa and walked around the room. She'd become restless and claustrophobic lately. "I think we should have gone for a judge."

"I only go for a judge when my client is very obviously innocent," he said, tracking her pacing with his eyes.

"But how can we pick the right jury?"

"We can't pick them at all. We take what we get, and then I work with them. Of course, we'll get our three peremptory challenges. I'll knock the biggest disasters off."

"What kind of jurors will you throw off?" she asked.

"Any real hard-core law and order types. Anyone with a son about the age of Benjamin Knapp. Redneck men who look like they might hate lady college professors. Any ugly women." He shrugged. "I'll have to see what we get."

"Ugly women?" she repeated. He sounded so harsh. "Why?"

"Because you're good-looking," he said with another little shrug.

She turned away. "If I had been uglier, maybe Benjamin never would have noticed me." Then she faced Keegan. "I think that's terrible. Is that what you think women are like? Just jealous and spiteful and willing to convict someone because they wish they were better looking?"

"That's right," he said. "They wouldn't admit it to themselves, but they might go in hoping you were guilty. We want them all to go in hoping you're innocent. I'd rather sell them what they want to buy than have to turn them around."

"It all sounds so capricious and arbitrary. I hate to admit it, because I've always believed in the jury system."

He made a little note in his pigskin-covered notebook. "Listen, in this case, a jury is what you want. I can work better that way. There are so many variables and nuances I can exploit. When I try a case in front of a judge, it's like playing the piano. When I work in front of a jury, I'm the conductor of an orchestra."

"I'm sure you'll be wonderful," she said. "I'm sorry if I've been a difficult client. I haven't always agreed with everything you've wanted to do, but I do respect your professional judgment."

"Well you'd better," he said sarcastically. "I'm one of the best goddamned criminal defense attorneys in the country."

She stiffened. "I didn't mean to sound pompous."

"You're no more difficult than any client who's got the threat of a long prison sentence hanging over him. But I sure wish I could convince you to change your plea."

"*No* way," she said sharply. "Confess to a crime I didn't commit? It's absurd."

"Okay, okay. We'll hit hard on the absence of a body. We'll do what we can with the expert witnesses. I don't think you realize how damaging that physical evidence is going to be. Most of all, we'll play down how you felt about Benjamin Knapp."

"And you still don't want me to testify?"

"Well, I could change my mind. It depends on what Applegate's planning. The prosecution's got a real problem. If they bring out Benjamin Knapp's behavior to you over the years, they establish motive, but they also create sympathy for you, and they make the victim unsympathetic. They might try to turn it all around, make you look nuts.

"If they do that, I might like to put you on and show them what a rational person you are. But if I do, and they ask you about Benjamin Knapp in cross, I'm afraid you won't be able to maintain the detachment from the victim that I want to establish."

"I don't think I could act like I didn't hate him," she said.

"Not even if it's the only thing to save you?" he said. "We're talking about prison. You want me to tell you what that's like?"

"No," she said quickly. "I'm not going to prison. I can't think that."

"Well you've got a good lawyer," he replied. "Now what did we decide you were going to wear?"

"That blue linen dress. You've already seen it."

He nodded. "Oh yeah. Pleats, right? Good. Remember, I want you to look demure and pretty and feminine. Dresses. Soft colors. Usually, I need to tell female defendants to tone down the sexy stuff, but in your case, I wish you'd do a little more. More makeup, anyway. And for God's sake, no suits or jackets. We'll probably have a slew of housewives on that jury, and they don't like career women."

She sighed. "I hope I don't have to testify. It really scares me. I've spent years explaining about Benjamin, and people don't believe me. It's so bizarre. I don't want to have to explain again." She looked at him searchingly. "You believe me, don't you? About all the things Benjamin's done?"

"That's the part I believe the most," he said.

Trevor Keegan had told her there'd be a lot of reporters and TV newspeople on the courthouse steps. He didn't tell her that they'd push forward and shout at her. She held on to Philip's arm and kept walking, trying not to look frightened. Ahead of them, Trevor Keegan had cleared a path and was now pausing to say into a microphone, "These charges should never have been filed. We expect a speedy acquittal, and then my client can go on with her life. This has been a nightmare for the poor woman."

When they came alongside him, he took Rebecca's other arm and leaned down to her solicitously. She looked into his craggy face and found herself almost sinking against him. Suddenly, after weeks of resenting Trevor Keegan, she felt a rush of feeling for him, gratitude, faith in his ability to take care of her, even affection. The feeling was so keen, she felt the beginning of tears.

His blue eyes narrowed analytically, then there was a flicker of comprehension, and he looked pleased and a little triumphant.

Ashamed of her feelings of dependence, she turned away and looked at Philip. "Thank you for coming," she said. "It means a lot to me."

"I think it's going to be all right," he said. "I really do, Rebecca."

Philip was wonderful, she thought. He always expected the best. She needed someone like that to balance her own dark streak.

In the courtroom, she sat and tried to look calm and gazed over at the prosecuting attorney. He was young and fresh-faced, with wavy red-gold hair. He was beautifully dressed. And he was staring at her. She wondered if he were trying to rattle her. She stared back, and he averted his eyes. It gave her some small satisfaction.

Next to her, Trevor Keegan arranged his pigskin notebook and a brand-new freshly sharpened pencil in front of him. Then he sat down and rubbed his palms together ever so lightly. She realized with a start that he was looking forward to her trial. He thought it was going to be fun.

"You do understand, don't you," said Trevor Keegan over and over again as he questioned each prospective juror, "that my client doesn't have to prove a thing? It's up to the state to prove its case. That's how we do things here in America, right?" The jurors would nod solemnly. "You believe, don't you, that my client is innocent until proven guilty?"

After a nervous glance in Rebecca's direction, they'd agree again. "You understand, I'm sure, that under our American system of justice — thank God — no one can be convicted if there's any reasonable doubt about his or her guilt?"

During the preparations for the trial, Rebecca had found his manner irritatingly casual at times. Now, as he questioned the members of the panel, his manner had changed. His voice was lower, the pace slowed down. His features assumed a heavy-lidded, tragic look. This trial, he seemed to be saying, was a trial of American justice itself. And the jury seemed to be taking it seriously. "You understand how grave the charge against my client is," he would say, pausing meaningfully and gazing intently at the prospective juror, "and how imperative it is that you fully appreciate the importance of the duty you are performing here."

By the time the jury box was full, all the faces turned toward him bore a reflection of his own solemnity.

When it was time for peremptory challenges, Rebecca looked over at his notebook. He had written down four numbers.

The first to go was a retired military man with a straight back and a grim set to his jaw. As he filed out, looking vaguely irritated that he'd been challenged, Keegan leaned over to Rebecca. "He'd convict the Virgin Mary," he whispered.

To no one's surprise, the prosecution then challenged a social worker with a soft, trembling face. She'd actually smiled sympathetically at Rebecca, who was sorry to see her go.

Keegan challenged a doctor's wife with a stiff blue-gray coiffure and a lot of jewelry. At the recess, Keegan had said she seemed rigid during the voir dire, and unlikely to follow a line of defense that relied on reasonable doubt. She also had a son about Benjamin's age and no daughters.

Applegate challenged an elderly man who'd been napping during the questioning of other jurors. "Too bad," said Keegan. "He might have come in handy on appeal."

There were two numbers left on the page. Rebecca glanced over at the jury. Juror number ten was a woman about her own age, heavyset with a shy, sallow face, who worked as a lab technician. Juror number seven, a phone operator, was a young girl who might have been pretty if she hadn't had a bad case of acne. It was clear Keegan wanted to challenge them because they weren't attractive. Rebecca felt somehow ashamed. She placed her finger on the number seven.

Juror number ten looked more sensitive and she was seated in the middle of a row. Rebecca couldn't bear to see her make a clumsy exit out of the jury box. Juror number seven sat at the end.

"Okay," said Keegan in a whisper, and then he rose. "We would like to excuse juror number seven," he said.

Rebecca looked over at them as they rearranged themselves. They all avoided her gaze. She couldn't tell much about them. It was like the first day of class when she looked out at the faces. Even after years of teaching, she was always a little nervous on the first day. The rows of faces always looked so blank.

11

"The state calls Michael Caruso."

Rebecca looked at him out of the corner of her eye as he walked up to the front of the courtroom. She didn't want to turn her head. He was maddeningly casual, strolling up to the stand, placing his hand on the Bible and touching the knot of his tie at the same time, something she noticed men often did before they spoke.

When he was seated, she allowed herself to look at him carefully. He looked back at her for just a second, and then his gaze flickered impersonally away.

"Mr. Caruso," began Applegate, "would you please tell the court what you do for a living?"

"I'm a private investigator." The jury looked pleased when they heard this.

"I see. And tell us, please, how you met the defendant, Rebecca Kendall." Applegate strolled around in front of the courtroom, looking, Rebecca thought, like an assistant professor giving a routine lecture.

"She came to me and asked me to do a job."

Keegan got to his feet. "Objection," he said in a voice that bristled with moral indignation. "Anything this witness could tell us would be privileged information."

"That's not true, Your Honor," said Applegate.

The judge, a bald, pink-looking man, excused the jury. They looked faintly annoyed as they filed out.

"Let's hear it, Mr. Keegan," said the judge.

"Mr. Caruso was acting as an agent of my defendant's then attorney, Angela Casaretti," said Keegan. "He was gathering information to help her in a matter in which Miss Casaretti was representing my client. It's very clear."

"And what do you say to that, Mr. Applegate?" said the judge.

"The defendant hired this witness directly. He presented her with a bill and she paid it. We will concede only that Miss Casaretti may have given the defendant directions to Mr. Caruso's office, but this does not constitute privilege. As Mr. Caruso is neither a priest, minister, or a lawyer, I don't see that Miss Kendall's communication with him can be construed as privileged in any way, regardless of whether or not he was her lawyer's agent."

"Objection overruled," said the judge, gesturing to the bailiff to summon the jury again. They filed back in, looking relieved to see that the private detective hadn't been whisked away during their absence.

When they had finished scraping their chairs and their feet, Mr. Applegate smiled reassuringly at them, as if to say "I'm glad you're back," and turned again to Michael Caruso. "Miss Kendall hired you to do a job," he repeated. "What was it?"

"She wanted me to find someone."

"Who was that, Mr. Caruso?"

"His name was Benjamin Knapp."

"I see. Did she say why she wanted to find him?"

"No."

"Did you ask her why?"

"Yes, I did. I like to know why I'm doing a job."

"I see. And what did she say?"

"She said she wanted to serve him with papers. Legal papers."

"And did you offer to serve him with these papers?"

"Yes, I did, but she said that wouldn't be necessary."

"Did she tell you what the nature of these papers was?"

"No."

"But you wanted to find out why she was looking for Benjamin Knapp, didn't you, Mr. Caruso?"

Keegan got to his feet and gave Applegate a withering glance. "Objection. Leading."

"I withdraw the question," said Applegate, pausing for a moment, then beginning again. "Did you make any further attempt to discover why Rebecca Kendall wanted to find Benjamin Knapp?"

"Yes, I did."

"And what did you find out?"

"She told me it was none of my business."

"And what was your reaction to that?"

"It irritated me. I like to know what I'm involved with. I've seen enough unhappy women in love to — "

"Objection," said Keegan, glowering. "The witness is making a reckless characterization of my client — "

"Try to answer the questions as directly as possible," said the judge. "Please continue."

Caruso frowned as if he was a little annoyed with himself. "I was afraid that Miss Kendall was emotionally involved with Benjamin Knapp in some destructive way. I tried to get her to tell me why she wanted to find him, and to counsel her to forget about him if necessary."

"I see," said Applegate. "How did she react?"

"She told me to back off."

"And did you?"

"Absolutely. It was clear she didn't want my help or advice."

Rebecca felt herself sneering. Help or advice. Caruso was trying to make himself sound like a social worker.

"Did you subsequently find Benjamin Knapp?"

"Yes, I did."

"And did you provide his home address and place of business to Miss Kendall?"

"Yes, I did."

"Over the phone?"

"No. In person."

"I see. And after Rebecca Kendall had that information, after she had the name and address of Benjamin Knapp, did she say anything to alarm you in any way?"

"Yes, she did."

"And what was that?"

"She said 'I wish I could kill him.' And she said any jury in the world would let her off."

There was an audible collective intake of breath throughout the courtroom. Carl Applegate paused, touched his cheek, and looked pensively at his wingtips as if mentally phrasing a question while the gasp hung heavily in the air. Keegan began clicking the locks on his briefcase and moving papers around as

116

if the witness's last statement wasn't damaging in the least.

"Now Mr. Caruso, could you tell the jury what you were doing on the night of March seventh of this year?"

"Yes. I was conducting a surveillance outside a bar in Alameda County."

"And after that, how late was it?"

"I was parked outside until two A.M. on the morning of the eighth."

"Then what did you do?"

"Then I drove to the address I'd given Miss Kendall. Benjamin Knapp's address."

"Why did you do that, Mr. Caruso?"

"Because the whole thing had made me uneasy. I wondered what kind of a person Benjamin Knapp was, and what kind of a house he had. I thought if I could see his house I'd have a better handle on why Miss Kendall wanted to find him." Caruso looked a little uncomfortable here, then concluded, "I had a bad feeling about the whole thing."

"And was this address 2667 Carlmont Circle?"

"Yes, it was."

"What did you see when you arrived at that address?"

"I saw that the front door was open."

"What did you do then?"

"I went up to the door and walked into the house."

"Why would you do that, Mr. Caruso? Walk into a strange house."

"I think it's because I used to be a policeman," said Caruso. "An open door at two A.M., that's usually a sign of trouble — a burglary or something. I checked it out, I guess, out of habit."

"I see. And what did you find inside the house?"

"I found a lot of blood. A whole lot of blood."

"Where was this blood, Mr. Caruso?"

"On the walls, on the floors, in the kitchen. But mostly it was on a mattress. The bed was soaked with blood."

"What did you do when you came upon this scene?"

"I called the police," said Caruso. He then described the arrival of the police, and made it clear he hadn't disturbed the scene in any way while he waited, and that, as a policeman, he had been trained to secure a crime scene.

"And did you ever see Rebecca Kendall again?" asked Applegate.

"Yes, I did."

"When was that?"

"It was later that morning. I went with the officers to her apartment."

"Why did you do that, Mr. Caruso?"

"They invited me. I was interested enough to go along. I had told them about Miss Kendall's threats — "

"Objection," said Keegan. "The witness is drawing a conclusion."

"The jury will disregard the word 'threats,'" said the judge. "You may continue, Mr. Caruso."

"I went along partly to identify her."

"I see. So you and the police officers proceeded to Miss Kendall's apartment."

"That's right. We picked up a San Francisco detective first, because we were out of their jurisdiction."

"Can you tell us what transpired when you and the detectives arrived at Miss Kendall's apartment?"

"The police asked Miss Kendall a few questions. Then they asked for permission to search her apartment."

"And what did she say?"

"She told them to go ahead and look around."

"She didn't ask for a warrant?"

"No. Her boyfriend wanted her to call a lawyer, but she didn't pay any attention to him. She gave her permission for a search."

"Thank you, Mr. Caruso," said Carl Applegate, permitting a small smile to cross his features. "Your witness, Mr. Keegan."

Trevor Keegan approached the witness slowly, then smiled at him. Caruso nodded his head a little in return, but he didn't smile.

"Mr. Caruso, I hope you'll bear with me. I want to go over your testimony, and make sure I understand all the details that make up the background of your story. Now, you've testified that Rebecca Kendall came to your office and asked for your help."

"That's right."

"She wanted you to find Benjamin Knapp for her, and you've told us you did." He turned slightly so the witness saw him in three-quarter profile.

"That's right," said Caruso.

"How did you do that, Mr. Caruso?"

"Well, it's a fairly routine matter," said Caruso.

"Please answer the question, Mr. Caruso."

Caruso shot Carl Applegate a pleading look and a second later, he was on his feet. "Objection," said Applegate. "Irrelevant."

The judge looked thoughtful. "Overruled," he said after a pause.

"Please answer the question," said Keegan pleasantly.

"I used a confidential source," said Caruso. "Someone who has an up-to-date listing of telephone company subscribers."

"And you gave this individual money and he gave you Benjamin Knapp's address?"

"That's right."

"Are you telling us that you bribed an employee of the telephone company, Mr. Caruso?"

Applegate rose again, but before he had a chance to object, Caruso answered the question. The corner of his mouth twitched slightly into a smile. "I have no way of knowing where my confidential source is employed," he said. "I only know that the information I get is invariably accurate."

Rebecca had hoped Keegan's line of questioning would make Caruso seem sleazy to the jury. But with that little half smile, Caruso had managed to look instead like a guy who knew his way around, and to make Keegan sound priggish for questioning his methods.

"All right, Mr. Caruso, let's go back before that. You've told us that you asked my client why she wanted to find Benjamin Knapp, and that she explained she wanted to serve him with papers."

"Correct."

"And then, Mr. Caruso, you've testified that rather than simply accepting this explanation, you persisted and pressed to discover the nature of the matter."

"Yes, I suppose I did."

"Why, Mr. Caruso? Why should you care? You can make money just paying off a person who might well be an employee of the phone company and passing that information along."

Applegate objected. "He's making a speech."

"Sustained."

Keegan continued, without missing a beat. "Why did you persist in trying to get my client to confide in you about a matter on which, presumably, she had already received legal advice?"

"It's hard to explain," Caruso said, glancing over at Rebecca. "I sensed some strong feeling there, and I couldn't put my finger on what it was. I wanted to know what motivated her."

"I see," said Keegan, in a tone that indicated he didn't. "You sensed some strong feeling. Then you testified Rebecca Kendall said she wished she could kill Benjamin Knapp."

"That's right."

"Did she say she was going to kill Benjamin Knapp?"

"No."

"Did she say she was going to try to kill Benjamin Knapp?"

"No."

"She said she wished she could, didn't she?

Isn't that what you testified to?"

"That's right."

"Doesn't that imply she knew she couldn't?"

"Objection. He's asking for a conclusion on the part of the witness," said Applegate.

"I withdraw the question," said Keegan. "Let me start again. My client said 'I wish I could kill him.' That's what you said."

"That's right."

"Are you sure she wasn't being facetious? Wasn't she saying" — Keegan clenched his fists and parodied a whine — "'I could just kill him.'"

"I didn't think she was being facetious. She seemed angry."

"Are you telling me you really believed she was going to kill Benjamin Knapp, this man upon whom she was planning to serve legal papers?"

"I was worried about it," said Caruso.

Keegan put his hand on the carved railing between him and Michael Caruso and bore down on the witness with his smoky blue eyes. "Don't you think, Mr. Caruso, that it was irresponsible of you to give her his address if you thought she was going to kill him?"

"I'd already given it to her."

"Well, then, shouldn't you have called the

123

police? Shouldn't you have called Mr. Knapp and warned him?"

"I didn't know my hunch was right until I saw the scene," said Caruso.

Keegan smiled. "Precisely my point, Mr. Caruso. You heard a chance remark, a flippant remark, and you did nothing. Then when you concluded, after snooping around Mr. Knapp's house, that something might have happened to him, you remembered that chance remark and you gave it ominous significance."

"Objection!" exclaimed Carl Applegate. "Mr. Keegan is making a speech."

"Save it for the summing up, please, Mr. Keegan," said the judge mildly.

"Are you a responsible person?" said Keegan now.

"Yes."

"Then I'm sure if you really thought Mr. Knapp was in danger, you would have warned him."

"I was uneasy," said Caruso.

"Did you have anything substantial to go on? I'm just trying to find out what evidence you really had. Answer the question, please, Mr. Caruso. You didn't warn Mr. Knapp because you had nothing to go on. Yes or no?"

"Nothing concrete, no. I just had a funny feeling. I didn't know where this woman was coming from. I usually do. It bothered me. A lot." He stared over at Rebecca.

"Ah," said Keegan sarcastically. "You met a woman you didn't understand? This doesn't usually happen to you. We'll take your word for it that you're an expert on women.

"Now, Mr. Caruso, let's go back to the time when you took it upon yourself to go over to Benjamin Knapp's house. You'd been conducting a surveillance in a bar, you testified."

"That's correct."

"I suppose that's what detectives do, Mr. Caruso. Hang around in bars looking to find stray husbands."

"Sometimes. But this was a collection matter."

"Did you enter the bar at any time, or were you outside, like in the movies, behind a newspaper?"

"I was in and out of the premises."

"Did you have anything to drink?"

"A couple of Scotches."

"And do you think your judgment was impaired in any way by those Scotches?"

"Not those Scotches. They were pretty watery," said Caruso with that half smile again. Rebecca looked over at the jury. She could tell a few of the women thought he was charming.

Keegan pressed on, getting Caruso to explain how he'd found the house and when he'd decided to enter. "And so you thought the place was a mess, that there'd been some sort of a struggle there, and you'd better call the police. Right?"

"Right."

"How long were you in that house alone, waiting for the police, Mr. Caruso?"

He shrugged. "Maybe twenty minutes."

"And can you swear, Mr. Caruso — remember, you're under oath — that you touched nothing, disturbed nothing at the scene?"

"Absolutely," replied Caruso.

"I see." Keegan managed to look dubious. "All right, I have just a few more questions, Mr. Caruso. Please be patient with me. I want the jury to have a complete picture. Now, when you went over to San Francisco and led the police to Rebecca Kendall, who was at the house?"

"A Mr. Philip Patterson."

"Miss Kendall's fiancé, correct?"

"I've learned since that he is, yes."

"Can you point him out?"

Caruso indicated Philip, sitting behind Rebecca. Philip put a hand on Rebecca's shoulder and she half turned and smiled gratefully at him. The jury stared over at them, fascinated.

"Didn't that blow away your theories about Miss Kendall? Weren't you surprised to see she had a fiancé, that she was a happy young woman?"

"I didn't have any theories about Miss Kendall. That was the problem. I didn't understand her reason for wanting to find Benjamin Knapp. Or why she hated him so much."

"Mr. Caruso, do you think my client is attractive?"

"Yes, I do," said Caruso, his brows rising in surprise.

"As a matter of fact, you told her so in your office, didn't you?"

"I don't think so. I may have. To cheer her up."

"Did you indicate to her that she was attractive enough to find another man?"

"Maybe. I did think it was too bad she was hung up on this Knapp character. I may have tried to let her know, gently, that she didn't need him, and it wasn't a good idea to stir up old pain."

"But Miss Kendall didn't want your advice, did she?"

"No, she didn't."

"She made that pretty clear, didn't she?"

"Yes."

"Be honest with yourself, Mr. Caruso, and

with this court and this jury. Are you sure you didn't resent the fact that Miss Kendall, a woman you found attractive, didn't want your advice? Are you sure you weren't bitter about that? Bitter enough to tell the police about a chance remark?"

"I'm sure," said Caruso, giving Rebecca a rather cool glance.

"I have just one more question, Mr. Caruso. When you were at Miss Kendall's apartment, and you heard her give the police permission to search her apartment, did she seem at all anxious? Did she seem frightened or anxious?"

"No."

"Did she seemed concerned at all?"

"No."

"Did she show fear of the police?"

"No."

"Was she reluctant to discuss the case with them?"

"No."

"Was she reluctant to allow a search of her home and her car?"

"No."

"Would you describe her demeanor for us, Mr. Caruso?"

"She was happy. She said it was because Benjamin Knapp was dead."

12

In the hall outside the courtroom, Caruso watched as Carl Applegate approached him. Applegate's thin skin was red in patches, and his cool courtroom manner seemed to be gone.

"God, thanks a lot," said Applegate. "We really appreciate your help."

Caruso waited, but Applegate didn't elaborate. Mildly irritated, Caruso said: "I guess you do. I managed to get that last damaging statement in during cross-examination. Did you forget about it, or what?"

Applegate paused for a moment, as if forming some dignified explanation, then shrugged. "I can't believe I forgot to ask you that last question. But it all turned out for the best, didn't it? It was more dramatic coming out in cross."

"Don't let Keegan rattle you," said Caruso casually, noting with satisfaction that the patronizing comment rattled Applegate a little more. "After all," he added, "he really screwed up in there. When he asked me about her attitude when she heard Knapp was dead, he knew she'd said she was glad he was dead. It was in the police report. Either he made a stupid mistake, which canceled out yours, or he's up to something pretty tricky. Which do you think it is, Applegate?"

Applegate shrugged, and tried to look nonchalant. Caruso laughed, and ran to catch the last elevator, stopping the door with his hand. As he got in, he saw that Rebecca Kendall, her fiancé, and her lawyer were all in the elevator. He nodded briefly and turned around quickly to face the front. He was struck by the glimpse he'd had of Rebecca Kendall's face. She hadn't looked mean or bitter at all. Nothing like she'd looked when she'd talked about Benjamin Knapp in his office that day. Of course, Keegan had her dressed in some flowered print dress with a lace collar. But it wasn't just the dress. It was her face. She looked soft and pale and helpless, with a kind of translucence to her skin and wariness in her eyes.

For the very first time, Michael Caruso felt sorry for her.

Several days later, Michael Caruso went back to court as a spectator. He'd resisted the impulse at first. He'd told himself to forget

130

about the Benjamin Knapp matter after his own testimony. He was irritated with himself, but he couldn't stay away. He supposed it was because he had to know whether by finding Benjamin Knapp, he'd served somehow as an instrument of his death. He'd told himself firmly that he wasn't responsible. It was Rebecca Kendall who'd made the choice, the choice to kill, and she bore the moral responsibility.

He'd missed the police testimony, but the gist of it was all over the newspapers and the TV news. They'd found human blood in the trunk of her car. It was pretty sensational stuff.

They'd also testified that she had given her permission for them to search her apartment and later her car.

He sat halfway back, near the center, and watched them swear in a cute, slightly plump redhead with artfully tousled hair.

She was sending out mixed messages, Caruso thought, noting the dark blue business suit that managed to show a long expanse of curvy leg ending in high, high heels. The witness was identified as Sandra Cunningham, chief of personnel at the insurance company where Benjamin Knapp had worked.

Caruso thought with amusement that she was thrilled to be testifying at a murder trial, but was managing to mask her enthusiasm with a fairly businesslike manner and a solemn, big-eyed expression.

Applegate took her through her paces, and she testified that Benjamin Knapp had been personally known to her, and that he was a quiet, responsible, conscientious employee, who worked in the computer services department.

"And do you recognize these papers?"

"Yes. That's Benjamin Knapp's personnel file."

"And do you recognize the signature at the bottom?"

"That's mine."

"Now take a look, will you please, at the medical portion."

Miss Cunningham flipped through the papers, and Applegate continued. "There seems to be a lot of medical data on these forms," he said. "Could you tell us why?"

"Well, each new employee takes a drug test. There is also some testing after employment, on a case-by-case basis. This file contains clinic results from Benjamin Knapp's drug tests."

"He was tested more than once?"

"Yes. A pre-hire test, and then another one six months ago."

"And the medical report from the clinic is

included in his file?"

"Yes, it is."

"Does it list Benjamin Knapp's blood type on those forms?"

"Yes it does," said Miss Cunningham, looking rather pleased with herself.

"And what is it?"

"O-positive."

"Thank you. Now, Miss Cunningham, could you tell us about Mr. Knapp's work habits? Was he out sick a lot?"

"No. He took three days of sick leave in three years," said Miss Cunningham.

"And did he call in and say where he was on those days?"

"Oh I imagine so. If he hadn't, there would probably be a notation in his file. Our company is quite conservative about that type of thing."

"So from what you knew personally about Benjamin Knapp, and what we know from this record, do you think it likely that Benjamin Knapp would just take off and not tell anyone?"

"No. I don't."

"And when did he come to work last?"

Miss Cunningham consulted her records. She had probably memorized the date, but didn't want to appear too eager, Caruso thought. "March second," she said.

"Did he call in sick?"

"No. We were very surprised."

"And has anyone at your company seen or heard from him since?"

"No, we haven't."

Keegan waived cross-examination, and Applegate presented his next witness, Dr. Trivedi, a forensic serologist. Applegate took Dr. Trivedi, a small East Indian man with a high-pitched voice, over his impressive academic credentials, and then asked him about the scene at 2667 Carlmont Circle.

"Can you describe what you found there, Doctor Trivedi?"

"A great deal of blood," he replied, and his rather chirpy accent made him sound cheerful about it. But then, mused Caruso, Trivedi was a blood specialist. Maybe the sight of a great deal of blood did cheer him up.

"How much blood, Doctor?"

"That is, of course, difficult to ascertain, but I was able to examine the mattress, in which most of the blood had been collected, and I estimate that there were at least six pints in the mattress."

"Six pints. And how did you make that estimate?"

"My assistants and I removed a portion of the mattress and were able to determine its rate of absorbency. Then we measured the

134

areas of the mattress that were saturated with blood." Dr. Trivedi spread out his brown hands. "A simple mathematical calculation was all that was required to arrive at the estimate."

"Doctor Trivedi, how much blood is there in the average body?"

"About five quarts."

"So six pints would represent more than half of the total?"

"That's right."

"Could anyone who lost that much blood live?"

"Oh, no." Dr. Trivedi looked shocked. "A man could bleed to death and lose a great deal less blood."

"And was there additional blood elsewhere?"

"Yes, on the walls in the bedroom, and on the kitchen floor and in a towel on the sink."

"Were you able to type this blood?"

"Yes. We took samples from the mattress and the towel, and from the sink. The blood was all human blood, type O-positive."

"Did the police show you other samples of blood in connection with this case?"

"Yes." The doctor nodded. "We also analyzed blood from the rug of an automobile."

Applegate held up a large plastic bag, opening it to reveal brown carpeting backed with rubber. "Is this the rug you examined?"

"It is."

"Let the record show the witness has identified Exhibit C, which police officers have testified they removed from the trunk of a Honda Civic belonging to Rebecca Kendall and parked at her residence on the morning of March eighth."

"What did you find on this rug?"

"More blood," said Dr. Trivedi happily.

"And was this blood analyzed?"

"Oh yes. We determined that it was also human blood. O-positive. This led us to analyze it further."

Here Dr. Trivedi's eyes lit up and he explained how modern blood-typing techniques made it possible to match samples with extreme accuracy. The doctor went on at some length, until the jurors became restive. Finally, Applegate cut him off.

"So what are the odds, Doctor, that the blood from the trunk of Miss Kendall's car, and the blood found in the mattress at 2667 Carlmont Circle were from the same individual?"

Dr. Trivedi beamed. "Over a billion to one," he said.

"Your witness," said Applegate, with just a trace of a smile of triumph.

"Thank you," said Keegan affably, his

manner showing no concern about the previous testimony. He rose and came toward the witness.

"Doctor Trivedi, tell us, will you please, what type of blood is the most common?"

"O-positive."

"And that's the type of blood you analyzed for the police here?"

"That's right."

"Doctor," Keegan said, puzzlement in his voice, "whose blood did you analyze?"

"I have no idea," said the doctor.

"It could be anyone, is that what you're saying?"

"That's right. But," the doctor held up an admonishing finger, "it is all from one individual."

Keegan waved that aside as inconsequential. "You've testified that this individual could not have lived and lost the amount of blood you found in the mattress, isn't that correct?"

"Yes."

"How did this person, whoever it was, die?"

"I do not know," replied the doctor, flashing beautiful white teeth in a wide smile.

"Could this person have died a natural death?"

Dr. Trivedi paused. "In the absence of a

body, it is naturally hard to say, but death was most likely caused one would think, by a wound, maybe even a decapitation or amputation."

Keegan looked surprised for just a moment, then his eyes narrowed. "Why do you say that?"

"Because of the enormous quantity of blood. With death, the heart stops pumping. For all that blood to have flowed into the mattress, the wound must have been large and strategically located to have allowed the blood to drain. The body too must have lain in a position to facilitate the flow of blood."

"Would the kind of wound you're describing require a great deal of strength to inflict?" said Keegan.

"Objection," said Applegate. "This line of questioning is highly speculative and you are asking the witness not only to venture opinions outside of his field of expertise, but to draw all sorts of conclusions."

"Sustained," said the judge.

"Were there any splatter marks on the walls or floors surrounding the mattress?"

"No, there were not."

"Splatter marks could have told you how whoever it was might have died — if he did in fact die, isn't that true?"

"Yes. There is a great deal to be learned

from blood splatter marks. Blood spurting from an aorta, for example, makes a characteristic pattern."

"But there were no splatter marks. So you don't even know if the person — whoever it was — who lost that blood was hurt in the location where the blood was found?"

"There were smears of blood on the walls that seemed to me to have been splatter marks that were smeared by a towel we found in the kitchen."

"Now let me get this straight, Doctor. Correct me if I'm wrong. You think someone died. You don't know who. You don't know when. You don't know where. You don't know how."

Applegate rose. "Objection. Counsel is badgering the witness."

"Wait for a response after asking each question, Mr. Keegan," said the judge.

"You don't know who died, do you?"

"No."

"And you don't know when they died, not even what day, do you?"

"No."

"Do you know how they died?"

"They lost a lot of blood."

"Could they have lost it after death?"

"It's not likely." He frowned. "I suppose it's theoretically possible."

"Do you know how they lost a lot of blood?"

"No."

"Do you know where they died?"

"I'm pretty sure they died on that mattress. That's where the blood was."

"Pretty sure? That's not good enough, Doctor."

He paused. "I'm absolutely certain. I can't imagine any other possibility."

"You can't imagine any other possibility," repeated Keegan with a touch of wistfulness. "Is this what it's about, Doctor? What you can imagine? The fact is, Doctor Trivedi, you really don't know how that blood got there or to whom it belonged originally, or really anything else about this affair, do you?"

"Objection," said Applegate. "Counsel is rephrasing questions that have been asked and answered. And in an abusive manner."

Before the judge could answer, Keegan waved his hand. "I withdraw the question." He looked pensive for a while, then turned slowly toward the witness. "I want you, Doctor Trivedi, as a man of science, as a fair man, as a thoughtful man, to answer me with complete honesty. Can you really say, from the scientific evidence, whether or not there is any real proof of murder?"

"From the scientific evidence alone? Strictly speaking, I cannot. But . . . "

"Thank you," said Keegan hastily, talking over the witness.

Dr. Trivedi, however, was determined to finish his thought. "But the absence of a body," he said, his voice rising a little, "is very suggestive of foul play."

13

"The State calls Evelyn Knapp."

Rebecca stiffened when she heard the name and watched warily as Benjamin's mother took the stand.

Evelyn Knapp looked much the same as she had some fifteen years ago when Benjamin had been on trial. Her face had the same ceramic quality — as if too much mobility and emotion would crack the surface. Her hair, which she'd worn swept up in a large iron-gray wave, rather like a cartoonish candle flame, was still the same odd shape. Now, however, it was white with a bluish cast. Once you looked beyond the careful makeup — blue eye shadow wings rising above sooty lashes, the tangerine mouth, arched taupe brows, cheekbones glistening with frosty orange — you could see Benjamin's face in hers.

"Look her right in the eye," Keegan had said. "I don't want that jury to see you flinch when you look at her. But you've got to appear sympathetic. Remember, no matter how misguided she is, she lost her son."

It was hard, however, to see Evelyn Knapp as a pathetic creature. Rebecca fixed her eyes on her, mindful of Keegan's admonition. Evelyn Knapp stared back at her, the tangerine mouth pulled down in disapproval, the brows drawn ever so slightly together. "Strange," thought Rebecca. "Fifteen years ago, she glared at me in court, eyes blazing, full of rage. Then, I was accusing him. Now, when she thinks I've killed him, she doesn't look angry at all."

But this time it was Rebecca who stood accused. She looked back at the witness. There was more than disapproval in the woman's face. There was triumph.

"Mrs. Knapp," began Applegate, as she smoothed her skirt and turned attentively to him. "I know this will be painful, and I want to thank you for coming today. But we do need your help, to find out the truth about Benjamin."

She fingered her pearls and dipped her head as if composing herself, the strange, stiff peak of hair remaining rigid. She held the pose for just a moment before Applegate began.

"When did you last see or speak with Benjamin, Mrs. Knapp?" He spoke very gently.

Mrs. Knapp looked up at him. "March the

first," she said. Her voice was one of those gin and gravel voices — low and rough, but with a cultivated drawl.

"And did he indicate to you, Mrs. Knapp, that he was planning on leaving his job or going away?"

"No. Not at all. He was very pleasant, very relaxed. He said he'd be coming over to see us soon. He was always a very attentive son."

"I'm sure that's true, Mrs. Knapp." Keegan shot Applegate a look of disgust, but didn't object. "Have you heard from him since he vanished, Mrs. Knapp?"

"No, of course not. I've had to face the worst." She turned and looked at Rebecca. "He's been taken from me." A tear began to glimmer in the corner of her eye.

"Mrs. Knapp, how long have you known about Rebecca Kendall?"

Her rigid form sagged just a little. "Let's see, I guess they had their first date about fifteen years ago. In college. Benjamin was just a freshman." She smiled wistfully. "He was only eighteen years old. Just a boy, really."

Rebecca felt as if she'd been kicked in the stomach. She felt again some of the fear she'd felt that night on the beach, as Benjamin held up the knife. It had been so cold and dark on the beach. She remembered the headlights of the oncoming cars in the blackness.

The rather quaint phrase "date" fell so easily from Mrs. Knapp's lips. It all sounded like some Norman Rockwell picture — two adolescents goggling at each other over their sodas. Rebecca gripped the table in front of her, then felt Keegan's hand on hers. She turned, surprised, and looked at his face. He kept his eyes on the witness, but gave Rebecca a quick glance out of the corner of his eye. She felt suddenly safer.

"And soon after that time, Miss Kendall and your son were involved in court proceedings, were they not?" Applegate continued.

"Yes," replied Mrs. Knapp. "Of course, Benjamin was completely absolved. The judge said that Rebecca was just a — "

"Objection," said Keegan forcefully. "Counsel is allowing his witness to ramble, and offer hearsay."

"Sustained," said the judge.

Applegate began again. "This was a criminal matter, wasn't it, Mrs. Knapp?"

"Benjamin wasn't a criminal. That was proven in court."

"But your son was accused of a crime, wasn't he?"

"That's right."

"What was he accused of?"

Mrs. Knapp pointed. "She accused him of

assault. He was acquitted and the judge said . . ."

"Objection," said Keegan. "On the same grounds as last time. This witness seems determined to introduce the judge's remarks as she remembers them into this trial. It's hearsay, plain and simple. If this other matter is to be brought up, let the record speak for itself.

"If it exists," he added with a smirk. Rebecca knew Keegan had tried to get a copy of the trial transcript. She'd been surprised that it no longer existed, but Keegan had said he'd have been surprised if it had. Apparently, if no one requested it, a copy wasn't made or even stored for very long.

"Oh, but it does exist," said Mrs. Knapp. She smiled a stiff, strained smile and opened her purse. "I've brought it. The judge's remarks are right here." She waved a couple of yellowing, dog-eared sheets of paper in the air.

"Just a moment please," said Applegate, turning slightly pink. He snatched the document from Mrs. Knapp, seemed to look it over, then said, "As Mr. Keegan has asked that the record speak for itself, I'm sure he'll have no objection if this witness reads the remarks made by the judge at the conclusion of People vs. Knapp into the record."

He handed the paper back to Mrs. Knapp.

Keegan rose. "I'm still waiting for a ruling on a previous objection. When that's sustained, I have another objection. In the meantime, I ask that the jury be excused."

The judge nodded to the bailiff to take the jury out. "Your objection, Mr. Keegan, is sustained," he said. "But I must warn you not to make any assumptions about rulings from this bench. Let's hear your latest objection."

"Your Honor, I object strenuously to this witness being allowed to bring in her own evidence and enter it into the record. It's preposterous. I've never even seen this document. It may well be prejudicial to my client, and it was never revealed to the defense. Mr. Applegate would have us believe it is also new to him. I hope that is true. I would hate to think he was trying to pull a fast one."

"Approach the bench, both of you." said the judge. He leaned down to Evelyn Knapp. "Let's see that," he said irritably. She handed it to him with a smile.

Rebecca tried not to appear too interested in the muted discussion between the judge and the two attorneys. She didn't want to seem less than confident. Instead, she forced herself to look for a moment at Evelyn Knapp, who was gazing out at the spectators, a strange half smile on her lips. The woman

147

must be insane, thought Rebecca. Her strange little smile was proof. But then Evelyn Knapp had always smiled. She'd always pretended everything was just fine. That Benjamin was normal. That his crazy obsession was no more serious than a lovers' tiff.

Rebecca remembered the weird cards she used to receive on her birthdays. Teddy bears and rabbits — cards you might send to a child — with little notes in Mrs. Knapp's perfectly formed handwriting. "Hope Benjamin will bring you by soon to see us," "Benjamin tells us how well you're doing in school," "Hope you and Benjamin patch things up, dear. He's so fond of you."

Those little greeting cards had never mentioned the fact that Rebecca had dragged him into court and charged him with assault. Mrs. Knapp had seemingly forgotten about the whole thing and bought wholesale into Benjamin's madness. But now her bitterness had resurfaced, and she was eager to remember Rebecca's old defeat.

Mrs. Knapp, reflected Rebecca, probably believed all the lies she told herself, all the lies about her only child. And why wasn't she grieving? She seemed to be enjoying testifying, sitting there, heavily madeup, smiling that frozen smile, preening like some vivid, vulgar bird.

Rebecca turned away in revulsion. Keegan must show the jury just what she was. In his cross-examination, he must bring out all the odd gaps in her logic, her inability to face the truth abut her son. Keegan could do it. She knew he could. He was harsh and abrupt and he could even be cruel. But he was smart. He knew human weakness and he could exploit it. Rebecca wanted him to demolish Mrs. Knapp on the stand.

Philip reached forward and touched her arm, startling her. She'd forgotten he was there. "What's going to happen?" he whispered. "What did the judge say? Will this hurt us?"

"Probably," she sighed. "What do you think of Mrs. Knapp?"

"Well you have to hand it to her," said Philip. "After what she's been through, she's pretty brave."

Rebecca gave him a horrified look. Then, out of the corner of her eye, she saw that her look had been intercepted. Michael Caruso was sitting among the spectators, watching her. What was he doing here? Rebecca felt suddenly alarmed. He was stalking her, just as Benjamin had. He had dragged her into this mess and now he was sitting watching her at the trial.

She couldn't get away. She had to come

here every day and allow this strange man to watch her. She grabbed Philip's hand and squeezed it tightly. She wanted Keegan to come back from the bench and sit next to her at the table. She felt so helpless she wanted to put her head down on the table and sob. But she took a deep breath and willed herself to glare back at Michael Caruso. He looked away.

She wasn't going to be afraid any more, she promised herself, no matter what they did to her. She had spent too many years afraid.

After all, Benjamin was dead. Nothing really bad could happen now — unless all men were like Benjamin. But they couldn't be. Philip was here, holding her hand.

She turned and smiled at him. "I think I'm cracking up," she said.

"Me too," he replied. "This is awfully stressful."

Just then the attorneys returned to their respective tables, and the judge spoke. "I have decided to allow this document to be entered into evidence. It is a notarized document, and I have no reason to doubt its authenticity. I have weighed the inconvenience to the defense of its not having been revealed before the trial against the jury's need to have as many pertinent facts available as possible. And, for the record, there is absolutely no evidence to indicate that Mr. Applegate was aware of this document, and there is no doubt in my mind that had he known of its existence he would have submitted it in the usual way."

The bailiff returned the jury to the courtroom, and Applegate strode briskly up to where Mrs. Knapp sat patiently, her hands folded in her lap, her legs crossed demurely at the ankle.

"Do you recogize this document?" he said, holding up the papers Rebecca had last seen Mrs. Knapp give the judge.

"Yes," she replied.

"Could you describe it?"

"It's the part of the trial transcript where the judge talked about the case."

"All right, Mrs. Knapp, perhaps you'd read us the remarks the judge made in that trial many years ago when Rebecca Kendall accused your son, Benjamin Knapp, of assault."

Mrs. Knapp smiled and reached into her purse for a pair of tortoiseshell half-moon glasses.

"Here's what he said," she announced. " 'I find the defendant, Benjamin Knapp, not guilty. I'd like to add that this case strikes me as a frivolous one in which we are asked to take the word of a single witness against the defendant, and to bring the full weight of the criminal justice system into a matter that appears to me to be simply an example of modern courtship gone awry.

" 'It is only the allegation that the young man may have displayed a knife that gives this case any credence at all, and I believe that the complaining witness may be reacting hysterically. There is certainly reasonable doubt in my mind that this knife was ever displayed.

" 'If young women are to dress provocatively, indulge in alcohol and perhaps in controlled substances, then get into cars with boys and go joyriding, well then what are we to expect but that boys will test the limits?

" 'To Miss Kendall I'd like to say, young lady, you were lucky this time. While I don't condone predatory behavior by young males, it has traditionally been, and for good biological reason, the young woman who sets the moral tone of any encounter. I hope this will be a lesson to you.' "

Mrs. Knapp primly removed her glasses. Rebecca felt her hands forming fists. She'd had to sit and listen to that same ridiculous speech fifteen years ago, and now she was hearing it again in Evelyn Knapp's unbearably smug tones.

She thought of a thousand things to tell Keegan at the break, before he cross-examined Mrs. Knapp. She'd tell him about the weird cards and letters. About the judge who made those remarks. He was dead now, but a few years after her trial he'd been hounded off the bench for letting off a rapist and blaming the victim. Rebecca knew if Keegan really had a go at her, he'd be able to get her to crack, to reveal herself as what she was — a woman who'd woven an entire fantasy together to explain her son's irrational behavior.

She fantasized conducting the cross-examination herself, a Portia-like heroine, calmly questioning. "Has your son, to your knowledge, ever had a normal relationship with a young woman? Did your son have any friends? Isn't it true, Mrs. Knapp, that you were your son's only friend? Are you aware of all the legal remedies Miss Kendall tried to get your son off her back, Mrs. Knapp? Isn't it true, Mrs. Knapp, that your son was maladjusted, that he always had trouble fitting in socially? Where is your husband, Mrs. Knapp? Isn't it true that he never believed Benjamin? That he disowned him? Isn't it true, Mrs. Knapp, that Benjamin was a monster? That you produced and raised a monster and that he's better off dead?"

Rebecca jerked herself back to reality. Evelyn Knapp was talking. "They always had a stormy relationship," she said. "Rebecca was a very passionate person. I think Benjamin was afraid of her intensity. He always said she seemed to want revenge. Even though she had been attracted to Benjamin, I think Rebecca hated men."

Rebecca leaned over and whispered to Keegan, "Are you going to let her get away with this?"

He reached for a legal pad, took out his fountain pen, and wrote, "Yes, I am. I'm not going to beat her up in front of that jury."

Rebecca seized the pen and wrote: "This woman is lying through her teeth. She's pathological."

"I know," he wrote. "I've seen the type."

"Well, can you break her down on cross-examination?" whispered Rebecca urgently.

Keegan wrote in his flourishing and bold hand on a yellow legal pad, "We'll waive cross-examination."

Later that day, after they'd broken for lunch and were eating in one of the expensive restaurants Keegan favored, Rebecca lost her temper completely, and cut loose. "You bastard," she hissed across the table, noticing but not caring that Philip was observing her with disapproval. "You've got to cross-examine that woman. You've got to."

"What for?" he returned sharply in a low voice. "So the jury can see me beat up some more on a mother who's just lost her son? I had to go after her on that goddamn transcript, and it made me look like the bad guy.

"Besides which, I've seen witnesses like her and they hang right in there. This one won't break. Rufus Choate, the legendary American nineteenth-century trial lawyer, said it flatly: 'Never cross-examine a woman.' And that's the kind of woman he had in mind. I've got a rule of my own: Never cross-examine the mother of the victim. I want her off that stand as soon as possible."

"But she's lying. She's saying horrible things. She acts as if Benjamin were normal."

"Listen, sweetheart," sneered Keegan. "You don't seem to get it. You're on trial here, not Benjamin Knapp. If the jury knew what hell he'd put you through, they'd have no choice but to convict you, because you've chosen to plead innocent. I've been forced to try and prevent them from knowing just what kind of a guy Benjamin Knapp was and how much he had it coming. Believe me, if they knew — if half of what you told me about him was true — they'd have to believe you killed him."

"You think I did it. You've never said it, and I've been too embarrassed to come out and ask you, but you think I did it."

"The veal marsala's great," said Keegan.

"Answer me," said Rebecca, trying not to

let her voice get loud.

"Hand me the wine list," said Keegan to Philip, who obliged. To Rebecca he said, "The worst lawyer in the world is the lawyer who believes his client is innocent. And I'm one of the best." He paused and then said snappishly, "If you didn't do it, who did?"

"I don't know," she said. "I hope to God *someone* did."

14

She set her fork down. "All along, I've felt as if Benjamin were somehow torturing me further. Maybe he is. Literally." Her voice grew more agitated, and she realized an idea had been forming in the back of her mind for some time. "I know it's fantastic, but it is *possible*. It's just the sort of thing Benjamin would do. He's killed someone and made it look like he's been murdered. He killed someone with his own blood type. And he's framed me by putting that blood in my trunk!"

"Why would he do that?" said Philip, looking ashen.

"Because he's crazy," said Rebecca. "Don't you know that by now? He's completely nuts, just like his damned mother. My God, Benjamin's alive. I just know it." She turned to Keegan. "Can't we tell the jury that? I know it's what happened."

"It's a pretty wild story," said Keegan. "I've already hammered away on reasonable doubt, the absence of a body. I'd rather suggest various possibilities than come forth with a specific one — one that might make us look bad later if we slip on a small point." He shook his head. "It's too damned weird. In essence, we're charging the victim with murder. We'd have to establish that the man was completely insane."

"But he is," said Rebecca. "I guarantee it."

"I've been concentrating on establishing that you don't have sufficient motive, so I've been downplaying Benjamin's peculiarities. For the kind of defense you're describing to work, I'd have to paint him as a full-blown, raving lunatic."

"But he was. Is," said Rebecca impatiently.

"That's not the point," said Keegan rather scornfully.

"But why would he do that?" said Philip. "Kill someone just to get enough blood to make it look like you killed him? It's bizarre."

Keegan shook his head. "It's *too* bizarre. I can't change my defense in midstream like this."

"Will you think about it?" said Rebecca. "Can't you do it my way? It's my fate that's at stake here."

"Exactly," said Keegan.

"You haven't answered me, Rebecca. Why would he do such a thing?" said Philip.

"Because he's obsessed," said Rebecca. "I

know this man. He's been making my life hell for years."

"But I thought he loved you," said Philip.

"Love? It's not love. He thinks he owns me. He's enraged that I won't cooperate. If he can't have me, he'll destroy me."

She turned back to Keegan. "There must be some experts in erotomania. There've been plenty of cases. Men stalking women for years, turning violent."

Keegan poured himself some wine. "Jesus Christ," he said. "The prosecution will be finished in a day or two. By then I've got to have a whole defense pulled together around this wild premise. Let me think about it over the weekend." He glanced up at her. "It would mean putting you on the stand. Can you handle that?"

"Of course," she said. "What a question. I'd be eager to tell my story."

"Yeah, but look at you. A while ago, you were mad as hell at me. You can come across like a pretty tough broad."

"I hope I am. I've had to be. With a man like Benjamin Knapp in my life, I would have crumpled up and died a long time ago if I weren't tough." Rebecca was rather surprised to hear herself say this. Lately she'd felt so passive. She'd seen herself on the television news looking pale and helpless, wearing those girlish dresses, being led in and out of court by Philip and Trevor Keegan. It had started as an act that Keegan had demanded, and it had become a reality, but now she felt as if she were shaking off that passivity. Perhaps it was because she thought she'd found a solution.

"Okay, okay," said Keegan. "You've had to be tough. But the jury just wants to know if you're tough enough to kill. If you go on the stand, I want you to be the limp, terrorized victim. Can you do that?"

"I'd be so ashamed," she said. "It wasn't easy to be brave when I was eighteen years old, but I did it. To pretend — " She slammed her open palm down on the table. "Don't you get it? I've never given in to Benjamin Knapp and I can't now."

"I'm not asking you to give in to Benjamin," said Keegan. "I'm asking you to give in to me." There was a kind of intimacy in the way he looked at her as he said it that made her realize, with a start, that she'd felt stirrings of attraction to Trevor Keegan. It was absurd, because she disliked him thoroughly. Was it because she needed him right now, needed him to save her?

"I can't give in to anyone," she said simply. She glanced over at Philip. "No one." She realized with a pang that she'd been on the brink of surrender even before all this had happened. She'd been willing to lean on Philip's shoulder, to relax for the first time in her life, to let a man she loved do some of the thinking for her.

But she knew now it had been a dangerous illusion. Look what had happened to her. She was more cornered, more alone than ever. It was some kind of punishment for daring to be dependent. She must never let down her guard again. Her relationship with Philip would have to be recast with these new insights in mind.

She put her hand on his and smiled rather tenderly at him. She'd wait until after the trial to talk to him. She wanted to make it work. Meanwhile, she loved him for standing by her, for coming to court every day. She had never expected that much loyalty, that much love.

It was later, in her apartment, that she said to him, "I was so happy thinking I'd found the answer. Why that blood was in my car. But now I'm not so sure I like my solution."

"It will be hard to prove," said Philip. He was helping her make dinner, standing next to her at the counter deftly chopping onions.

"It's not that," she said. "Trevor Keegan, bastard though he is, is a good lawyer. It's that, well, I was kind of pleased, despite all I've been through, because I thought Benjamin was dead. If he's still alive, God, Philip, I don't know. I don't want to get scared again." She felt tears in her eyes and turned away.

He went to her side and took her in his arms. "It's a good thing I've been staying with you here every night," he said.

She pulled away. "It's all right, Philip, really it is."

"But you're crying," he said. "You're scared."

"No, I'm not. I'm not scared. And I'm not cryng, either. It's just the onions." She managed a rueful little smile and pulled away. Inwardly, she congratulated herself for having resisted the temptation to fall helplessly against Philip's shoulder.

Rebecca decided not to call Keegan over the weekend to urge him to change his defense, but it was one of the hardest things she'd ever done. She felt convinced her hunch was right and saw no reason why it wouldn't make a logical defense. It was the only way to explain the blood in the trunk of her car — the blood that perfectly matched the blood in the mattress at Benjamin's house.

It was the only scenario that fit in with the physical evidence and with what she knew of Benjamin Knapp. While it was a highly improbable solution, it was possible. In fact, it was the only possible solution that fit the facts as she knew them.

But she respected Keegan's knowledge of a jury — what they would buy and what they wouldn't — too much to tell him what to do. And he would have to present the story. Only he could decide whether or not he could do so convincingly.

By Monday morning, when she hadn't heard, she'd decided he wouldn't do it. It was a bizarre story. If only she could get across to everyone just how strange Benjamin Knapp could be. How could Keegan understand? How could he make a jury understand? Even Philip could never really know what she'd been through. No one ever would.

She was dressed and ready to go and waiting for the limousine Keegan had sent to her apartment to bring her to court every morning. Today, the first day of the defense arguments, she had rebelled. Instead of one of those demure dresses Keegan had picked out, Rebecca wore a severe straight dark skirt and a white silk shirt. No one could object to that, surely. She felt more like herself.

At first, the limousine had seemed ridiculous. She and Philip and Keegan emerged into the cameras every day like a bunch of movie stars. But after the strain of the trial, she had decided that luxury and privacy made a big difference in her attitude. And the sheer logistics of providing her own transportation when the cameras were outside every day would have been impossible. Keegan, of course, liked the flourish it gave his arrival.

Today, she was surprised to see Keegan already inside. Usually, the driver picked her up first, then swung by to get Philip if he had gone in to his office before court, as he had today, and then Trevor Keegan at his office.

"Good morning, my dear," he said, running an eye over her outfit. "That's okay for today, but I want something fluffier tomorrow."

She sighed. "God, I'm paying you a lot to insult me," she said, swinging her legs into the car and stretching them luxuriously out in front of her.

He laughed. "You won't mind when you get acquitted," he said. "You'll think I'm the greatest guy in the world."

She looked at him sharply. "I suppose all your female clients fall in love with you," she said with a trace of a sneer. "They're so grateful."

"That's right," he said complacently. "But it's worse for the divorce guys.

"Listen, I've thought about our strategy. I've worked all weekend on changing it along

164

the lines you suggested. I've been over all the physical evidence. Some of it is very support- ive, and I've got a line on a couple of expert witnesses. I'm thinking very seriously of pitching the idea that Knapp disappeared vol- untarily.

"By the way," he added, "I checked, and Knapp took off the day after payday. We'll see if he cashed his check. They usually do that, disappear with a full paycheck." He laughed.

"You're talking as if you believe my story," she said, surprised and pleased. "You really believe me, don't you?"

"It doesn't matter what I think," he said. "It matters what the jury thinks. Anyway, our first witness today is Angela Casaretti. I called her over the weekend and went over her testi- mony with her. Originally, I wanted her only to establish that you had a legitimate reason to have this Caruso character find Knapp.

"Now, I plan to have her go over the whole history of your involvement with Benjamin Knapp. She was there from the beginning, back at Stanford. It'll work out fine. Mean- while, my associates will have time to round up those expert witnesses. I shouldn't have any trouble introducing new material," he added confidently. "After all, the judge let Applegate skewer us with that transcript."

He gazed out the window for a moment. "It's a pretty weird story," he said. "But it's the only one I can think of that both explains the blood in your car and keeps you out of the slammer."

15

"The defense calls Angela Casaretti."

Caruso did a fair amount of business with the small law firm for which Angela Casaretti worked, and because that firm was in the same building, he ran into her a lot in the lobby and the elevator. She seemed like a no-nonsense, direct person. She always walked down the hall taking big steps, her long stride emphasized by her clothes: unlawyerly big skirts, boots, long cardigans. She was casually sloppy with a cloud of dark hair in corkscrew curls.

Today in court, Caruso was surprised to see her looking more subdued. The dark mane of hair was caught back and she wore a gray skirt and a navy jacket.

"You have been Miss Kendall's attorney in the past, have you not?" began Keegan.

"Yes," said Angela.

"And she has waived her attorney-client privilege?"

"Yes, she has."

"Could you describe the work you were doing for her on March the first, when she came to your office?"

"I had planned to get an injunction against Benjamin Knapp. He had sent a threatening telegram to her fiancé."

"Were you surprised to hear this?"

"Oh, no. I had been representing Miss Kendall in her attempts to protect herself from Mr. Knapp's harassment for years."

"And to serve Mr. Knapp with papers, you had to find out where he was, didn't you?"

"That's right."

"Objection, Your Honor," said Applegate, "counsel is leading the witness."

"Sustained."

Keegan continued, without faltering. "How did you suggest that Mr. Knapp be found?"

"We generally use a private detective, Michael Caruso, for matters like this. I asked Rebecca to drop by his office on her way out of the building and arrange to have Mr. Caruso find Mr. Knapp."

"Now, could you describe Miss Kendall's state of mind when she came to you and told you she wanted these papers served and that Benjamin Knapp had sent this telegram to her fiancé?"

"Objection," said Applegate. "This is outside the realm of this witness's expertise."

"Overruled."

Keegan continued. "Go ahead, Miss Casa-retti."

"She was naturally unhappy, because she'd thought her problems with Mr. Knapp were over. She was protective of her fiancé and wanted to spare him unpleasantness. But she was happier than I'd seen her in years. She was engaged and in love, and that loomed larger in her mind than Benjamin Knapp, I would say."

"Was she enraged?"

"No."

"Was she distraught?"

"No."

"Did she look like a woman with the urge to kill?"

"No."

"You've known Miss Kendall a long time, haven't you?" said Keegan.

Applegate got to his feet. "Objection, Your Honor. Counsel is again leading the witness."

"Sustained."

Rolling his eyes as if to let the jury know he thought Applegate's objection was petty, Keegan rephrased the question. "How long have you known the defendant?"

Angela smiled over at Rebecca. "Fifteen years. We were both freshman at Stanford, and we lived in Roble Hall."

"And can you tell us about the night Miss Kendall first met Benjamin Knapp, the alleged victim in this case?"

"Yes, I can."

"Describe that evening for us, if you can."

"It was late at night. I was in my room, which was next to Rebecca's. My roommate and I were both up, talking and listening to records. We'd been to the movies, I remember. And then Rebecca's roommate came and pounded on our door. I don't remember her name, but she was Rebecca's roommate."

"Why did she do that?"

"She was very upset and frightened. She asked us to come and help Rebecca. We went next door and saw Rebecca. She was sitting on a straight-backed chair in the middle of the room, kind of doubled over, her hands wrapped around her knees. And she was sobbing and rocking back and forth. I remember it quite vividly. She was wearing a white dress."

"She was in pretty bad shape emotionally? She'd been frightened badly?"

"Objection," said Applegate. "Counsel is leading the witness."

"Rephrase the question, Mr. Keegan," said the judge.

"How would you describe Rebecca Kendall's emotional state?"

"She was terrified," said Angela firmly.

"And was it your understanding that she had been abducted?"

"Objection!" said Applegate. "Leading. And this whole line of questioning is based on hearsay."

"Sustained," said the judge. "Rephrase the question and go carefully here. This entire line of questioning is at the edge, I would say, but I will allow it, providing you proceed with caution."

"Why, as you understood it, was Rebecca Kendall terrified?"

"She'd been at a party. The girl she went with had left her without a ride, but had arranged for Benjamin Knapp to drive her back to campus. He drove her to a secluded beach, refused to take her back to campus, struggled with her, struck her, allegedly displayed a knife, and forced her to partially disrobe."

Applegate rose to object, then sat down again, looking puzzled. Keegan had caught it out of the corner of his eye. He gave Applegate a little smirk as he continued with his questioning. From where he sat among the spectators, Michael Caruso caught the little interplay between the two men. What was Keegan up to? He seemed to be setting up his client's motivation to have killed Benjamin Knapp. One thing was clear. Applegate didn't know what Keegan was up to either.

"And how old were you and Rebecca Kendall at the time? You said you were freshmen?"

"Eighteen or nineteen."

"Did you go with Rebecca the next day to the police?"

"Yes. I urged her to file a complaint. She was frightened, but she was angry too, and finally she decided she should. We went to the campus police, but they said it hadn't happened on campus and they weren't interested, so we went to the Santa Clara County Sheriff's Office."

"And they took the complaint seriously?"

"Not at first. But I convinced them."

Keegan smiled. "Your natural talents as an advocate, Miss Casaretti, had already come to the fore."

While Rebecca Kendall was at Stanford, Michael Caruso reflected, he had been a police science major at San Jose State. It was only a few miles away.

"Let's go forward in time, now," said Keegan, leapfrogging over Benjamin's trial. "When did you pass the bar?"

"In 1975."

"And was Rebecca Kendall one of your first clients?"

"Yes. She consulted me in connection with

Benjamin Knapp."

"Do you recognize this file?" He held up a thick file folder.

"Yes. It's my file. It contains everything pertaining to Rebecca Kendall's continuing efforts to seek protection from the frightening and unwanted attentions of Benjamin Knapp."

"I object to this witness's flamboyant characterization of these documents," said Applegate. "As the witness is an attorney, it may be tempting for her to address the jury, but she is appearing as a witness."

"Just answer the questions, please," said the judge mildly.

"Can you identify this document?" asked Keegan, holding up the topmost piece of paper.

"That's a letter he sent her soon after he was acquitted." Applegate and the judge examined the document too. While they were reading it, Caruso watched Rebecca Kendall. She looked a little tougher today. Maybe it was what she was wearing. Maybe it was because the defense had begun its case.

She looked quite cool and self-possessed. Her dark blonde hair was twisted and pinned back. She might have looked like a schoolmarm if it hadn't been for the tendrils of hair that had escaped and curled around her forehead and at the nape of her neck, which looked surprisingly white and soft. To Caruso, it seemed that despite her present aura of confidence, the back of her neck spoke of vulnerability.

Keegan moved to have the letter admitted into evidence. Applegate, frowning and looking a little ill at ease, had no objection.

"Could you read this letter?" Keegan said to Angela.

Angela read the first of Benjamin's letters.

Dear Rebecca,

I want you to know, my darling, that I forgive you for calling the police. Now that the trial is over, and it's been proven I didn't hurt you in any way, I expect you'll see how dumb you've been about the whole thing.

You know as well as I do that we belong together, that we'll always belong together, and that to pretend otherwise is just to cause trouble and fight our mutual destiny.

I just wrote that we belong together. That's not really right, Rebecca. We belong to each other, and we always will, when we're together or apart. But there's no reason for us to be apart. Ever again.

Love, Benjamin

One by one, Keegan had the letters from the file admitted into evidence. One by one, Angela read them. Each one was a little harsher, lashing out at Rebecca for not responding. Finally, he'd come out and threatened her.

Dear Rebecca,

You can't get it through your pretty little head, can you? Well you will, if I have to pound it into your brain. You belong to me. And no one can take from me what is mine. Even you.

I'm coming over to see you this weekend, and I expect you to be there, and to be nice to me. I don't appreciate your hanging up on me like you did yesterday. I don't want to have to hurt you, Rebecca. I never have. The judge said so. But if I have to, I will. It's for our own good.

"Was your file complete?" said Keegan. "I mean, was every letter he sent her in here?"

"Oh, no. I tried to get her to keep them for our purposes, but she destroyed a lot of them unopened. As I recall she received three or four a week the first year after his trial.

"Later, she had the post office return them unopened. That finally worked. It made him mad, but he stopped writing. And of course, by then, we'd restrained him legally."

"I see. What's this document?"

"Oh, that's a telephone log. I asked Rebecca to keep track of the calls she received from him."

"And did she get an unlisted number?"

"Oh yes. Many times. He always seemed to get her unlisted number."

"The state's witness, Mr. Caruso, could probably tell us how he did that," said Mr. Keegan.

"Objection!" said Applegate, scowling.

"I withdraw my remark," said Keegan. "Would you identify this document, please, Miss Casaretti?"

She squinted at it for a moment. "Oh. This appears to be a letter from Mr. Knapp's attorney. It says his client categorically denies harassing my client, and that the restraining order we obtained was based on false assertions by Misss Kendall.

"The attorney reminds me that Benjamin was acquitted and is considering measures to make sure Rebecca does not continue to harass him with unfounded charges." Angela's expression let the jury know what she thought of the letter.

"What's the date on that letter?"

"This is 1979."

"So we're now into four years of legal skirmishing with Benjamin Knapp, is that correct?"

"Yes."

"Did he ever give up, Miss Casaretti?"

"There were quiet periods, but Mr. Knapp never gave up, no."

"If you'll bear with me, Miss Casaretti, let us proceed through this file. Could you identify this next item?"

A kind of numbness hung over the courtroom. The cumulative effect of the documents — letters from Benjamin, memos, other correspondence — read clearly and firmly by Angela Casaretti was staggering, Caruso thought.

It appeared that Benjamin Knapp had ground away at Rebecca Kendall for years. Sometimes there had been frightening episodes. Benjamin following her in his car on a lonely road. A neighbor spotting a man who sounded like Benjamin on a fire escape outside her apartment.

There had been small acts of vandalism too. Her car door scratched with a heart one Valentine's Day. Flowers from another man, left on her doorstep by the florist, shredded to pieces. Her mail apparently tampered with. Angela Casaretti phrased everything carefully, and made it clear that nothing was ever

177

proven. But her expression and tone of voice made it clear that there was no doubt in her mind that Benjamin Knapp had made her friend's life hell. Caruso glanced over at the jury. A couple of them were looking sympathetically at Rebecca. You couldn't help but feel sorry for her. But Caruso was confused. She had pled innocent. Now her lawyer was busy establishing motive. And Applegate was sitting quietly at his table, remaining silent as his opponent appeared to be hanging his own client. Despite his calm demeanor, Caruso imagined Applegate was scared to death. What was Keegan up to?

He'd sure made a good case for the prosecution. In fact, after what Rebecca Kendall had been through, Caruso wondered why she hadn't killed him sooner.

Or why some boyfriend hadn't. But reading between the lines in all the documents, Caruso got the impression that there hadn't been much of anyone. And now, in her mid-thirties, she was engaged, presumably for the first time. He looked over at Philip Patterson. Did he have what it would have taken to kill Benjamin Knapp?

16

"Your witness." Keegan turned away from Angela Casaretti. Her testimony had taken two days. Rebecca felt she had made a good impression. Angela seemed very straightforward and businesslike, but with an undercurrent of indignation on Rebecca's behalf, and in possession of all the facts.

"I'll just ask you a few questions," said Applegate, pacing his characteristic half circle in front of the stand. "Let us go back," he said, "to the time you were an undergraduate and you accompanied Miss Kendall to the Santa Clara County Sheriff's Office. You told us that at first the police were reluctant to investigate the incident in which Miss Kendall claimed Benjamin Knapp attacked her."

"That's right."

"In fact, you said you had to talk them into it. Opposing counsel congratulated you on your youthful powers of persuasion."

Angela tilted her head back a little and watched Applegate warily from below lowered lids. She didn't answer.

"My question is this — what reasons did they give for not wanting to bother with this case?"

"They said it was hard to prove. Her word against his."

"Did they say she hadn't really been hurt?"

"Yes, they said that. I didn't agree."

"You were present at that trial — People vs. Knapp — were you not?"

"Yes."

"Did the judge say she hadn't been hurt?"

"That seemed to be his attitude."

"In all the time you've represented Miss Kendall, have you ever alleged that Mr. Knapp harmed Miss Kendall in any way?"

"Yes, we have."

"In any physical way," he amended quickly.

"Not in any physical way, no." She managed to load her answer with as much innuendo as possible.

"So the answer is no. He never harmed her physically."

"Correct."

"I've had a chance to examine this file we've been discussing for the past two days, and one thing strikes me about these letters Benjamin Knapp is supposed to have written your client. Would you look again and tell me if you notice anything about them that makes them different from normal correspondence?"

She looked over the letters. "Other than that their content reveals Mr. Knapp to be a person obsessed, I see nothing remarkable about them," she replied.

"Are they signed?"

"Oh. That. No. He always typed them and typed in the signature. We thought it was because . . . "

"You've answered the question, Miss Casaretti. So there's no absolute proof that Mr. Knapp wrote these letters?"

"That was never at issue, so no absolute proof was ever sought."

"In fact, through his attorney, Mr. Knapp denied having harassed your client in any way. You examined and paraphrased a letter from your own files that made that clear, didn't you?"

"Yes, I did."

"So we don't know, do we, whether Miss Kendall's assertions that she was being harassed are true, do we?"

"There is no doubt in my mind," said Angela.

"In fact, the issue was brought into court one time many years ago. You've told us you were present at that trial. Tell us now what the verdict was. Was Benjamin Knapp found guilty?"

"No."

"How did the court find in the matter of People vs. Knapp, Miss Casaretti?"

"Objection. Asked and answered," said Keegan.

"Sustained."

"But we do know one thing for sure, don't we?" continued Applegate. "We do know that whatever Benjamin Knapp may have done, Rebecca Kendall continued to accuse him, long after he was acquitted. She continued to insist that he was harassing her and that she needed protection from him, didn't she?"

"She availed herself of legal remedies in trying to rid herself of him, yes."

"Trying to rid herself of him?" repeated Applegate.

Angela paled a little.

"Of what other remedies did she avail herself to, as you say, 'rid herself' of him?"

"None."

"How do you know that? Have you been with her twenty-four hours a day since college?"

"Of course not," snapped Angela.

"So you can't say for certain what means Miss Kendall may have used to rid herself of him?"

"Rebecca would never resort to violence. It's that simple," said Angela heatedly.

"Yet when the police told Miss Kendall

that Benjamin Knapp was dead, she expressed happiness."

"I don't know. I wasn't there."

"How many times over the years did she consult you about him?"

"Dozens."

"As an attorney, have you had dealings with clients who become preoccupied with a lawsuit, or who keep on pursuing a matter even when it doesn't make sense? Just because they get so caught up in it?"

"All lawyers have encountered the kind of client you describe," said Angela.

"Didn't it ever occur to you, Miss Casaretti, that Rebecca Kendall was such a client?"

"No it didn't," she said, then she rephrased it more firmly. "Absolutely not."

"You were with Rebecca Kendall on her first day in court. You were with her when the judge announced his verdict in People vs. Knapp, weren't you?"

"Yes."

"What was Rebecca Kendall's attitude when she lost? When the judge refused to believe her? When he said maybe she'd been lucky?"

"She was upset, naturally."

"She was bitter, wasn't she?"

"At first she was simply stunned."

183

"Ah! At first. And after that?"

"Rebecca Kendall has stood up to this very bravely over the years."

"I'm asking if Rebecca Kendall developed a bitterness, a hatred over the years."

Angela glanced over at Rebecca. "I don't think so," she said.

"You don't think so," repeated Applegate in a leaden tone. "Did she ever indicate that she'd like to hurt Benjamin Knapp in any way?"

"Only facetiously."

"Maybe you can tell us what she said."

"I object," said Keegan. "The witness has already indicated the remarks were humorous ones not to be taken seriously."

Applegate shot him a hostile look over his shoulder. "Your Honor, the defendant's expressed desire to do harm to the victim is relevant. It's up to the jury to decide the facts — in this case how the defendant intended such remarks."

"Overruled."

"Answer the question, please," said Applegate.

"I can't remember exactly. We both joked about it on occasion. Gallows humor," she complied, then stopped, looking horrified at what she had said.

"Did any of Miss Kendall's remarks have to

do with killing Mr. Knapp?"

"Well, they had to do with him being out of her life. Vanishing from the face of the earth. Falling off cliffs. I can't remember. We both made remarks like that." She threw up her hands in a flustered gesture.

"I am not asking you what you said. What did Miss Kendall say?"

"She said she'd like to see Benjamin dead."

"Did she say she'd like to cause his death?"

"Oh, sure. But kidding around. You know. 'I could kill him,' that kind of thing." Angela had managed to take on a lighter tone now.

"I have one last question," said Applegate. "In all the years you've known Rebecca Kendall, has she ever to your knowledge, forgiven him for whatever it was that is supposed to have happened on that beach fifteen years ago?"

"She just wanted him to leave her alone," said Angela.

"No further questions."

Keegan had just two questions on redirect. "Miss Casaretti," he said, "why do you think Mr. Knapp never signed his letters? Always typed them?"

"Benjamin Knapp had been frightened by his indictment after he assaulted Rebecca. After that, he was always extremely careful never to do anything we could get him on in a

185

court of law. He never admitted his obsession in any way that we could use against him."

"So you would say Benjamin Knapp was a crafty person?"

"Absolutely. That's what was so maddening. You could never pin him down. He thought out everything to the last niggling little detail. He was very, very sneaky."

On recross, Applegate asked her one question. "You said Mr. Knapp was a crafty person. In all your years of tryng to help Miss Kendall, none of your efforts ever really succeeded, did they? She never did rid herself of him using legal means, did she?"

"Not for long, no."

17

Rebecca was relieved that Keegan had business to attend to at noon and that she and Philip could be alone at lunch.

"I've got a surprise for you," he said in the hall. "I arranged it with Keegan. God, that man runs our whole life these days, doesn't he? It's like he's a parent."

"What's the surprise?" said Rebecca, feeling suddenly lighthearted."

"You'll see." He took her by the hand and they went outside into the sunshine. The light hurt her eyes at first, then she saw Keegan's limousine sitting at the curb.

"I'm taking you away from all this," he said, leading her to the waiting car. Inside was a massive wicker picnic hamper and a bottle of still white wine chilling in a bucket of ice.

"A picnic!" said Rebecca. "How could you think of such a thing? We've been so worn down by all this."

"It's true, we haven't had a whole lot of fun lately," he said wryly, tapping on the glass.

"When we got engaged, I never knew how much trouble you'd be, Miss Kendall." As the car entered traffic, he produced two wineglasses from the hamper.

"Where are we going?"

"Oh, I know a secluded little park up in the Berkeley Hills. Time's a little short, though. We'd better have our aperitif now." He opened the wine bottle and poured them each a glass. "I thought champagne would be a little showy," he said. "Too much like the senior prom."

"Let's save it for the victory celebration."

"You're feeling more confident now, aren't you?" he said.

She tasted the wine. It was delicious. "Yes. Of course. Aren't you? I feel better about everything. I'm sure Keegan can convince them. But let's not talk about it at all."

She leaned her head back against the upholstery and looked out the window as the car worked its way up curvy streets past pleasant old houses that looked as if generations of dull, happy families had lived in them. How wonderful that seemed.

When they arrived at a quiet park in a residential district, Philip wrestled the hamper out of the car, consulted his watch, and instructed the driver to come back in forty minutes.

He spread out a blanket and unpacked the hamper, while Rebecca sat and marveled at the collection of delicacies inside — cold chicken, cucumber sandwiches, a salad of tomatoes and olives, green grapes, a delicately flavored white cheese and chocolate-covered strawberries.

She looked around her at the small grassy patch, the blue sky, two gnarled, grayish California oaks, and a nearby stand of eucalyptus. It was quiet, except for the lazy sounds of bees. She realized how claustrophobic she'd felt in court, and she dreaded going back there this afternoon.

Philip sat next to her, stroked her hair, refilled her glass. She closed her eyes and felt sunshine on her eyelids. "Oh, Philip, thank you," she said. "It's all so much more precious to me all of a sudden. The sky, the trees, the strawberries. Philip, I hadn't really thought about it until now. If we lose — if I go to prison —"

"That won't happen," he said softly. "Even if you get a guilty verdict, there's always the appeal. I wouldn't even think about it for a long time."

"You don't think they'd find me guilty, do you?" she said. "Tell me the truth."

"Do you think I believe that for a minute?" he said. "I don't think I'd be here if I thought that. Besides, I'm testifying this afternoon. That jury will see that if you're free you can marry a prince and live happily ever after. How can they resist?"

That afternoon, however, before Philip began his testimony, Carl Applegate asked for permission to address the court.

Rebecca noticed that the fair-skinned prosecutor had pink splotches on his neck and face. "Your Honor," he began, "at this time, because of new evidence that has just been brought to my attention during the noon recess, I must ask to reopen my case."

18

Caruso had been sitting forward in his seat, watching Rebecca Kendall and Philip Patterson. They had come in looking animated and flushed like a couple in love. But there was something a little too attractive about them, he thought. Or maybe it was that they resembled each other too much, with similar coloring and a kind of golden, carefree look. How they could be carefree under the circumstances, he couldn't imagine. But then, they had to be crazy. After all, she was probably a cold-blooded killer, and he was too dumb to know or care.

When Applegate had announced that he wanted to reopen his case, Rebecca's face had drained of color. She had stared at her own lawyer with a look of incomprehension.

The jury was excused, the attorneys and the judge repaired to chambers, the spectators whispered, and Rebecca Kendall sat bolt upright and pale.

It seemed like half an hour later when the

judge and the two attorneys returned. Caruso could tell that Applegate had been allowed to reopen the case. He entered the courtroom with a barely disguised smile and a spring to his step. Keegan, on the other hand, looked like he wanted to kill. And he looked like he wanted to kill his client.

Caruso watched their hasty, whispered conference. Philip Patterson leaned forward, listening, but they seemed to be ignoring him. Caruso could see the back of Keegan's immaculately barbered silver head and one hand, folded almost into a fist, gesturing in the air.

He was waving that hand so close to Rebecca Kendall's face she blinked, but she didn't move. As she listened, Caruso saw her eyes widen — with surprise or fear he couldn't say. He even heard her voice in normal tones emerging from the whispers. "No," she said, "Never."

Before the jury came back, the judge spoke. "Because there is some question as to why this witness has not appeared sooner, because the state has waited until now to introduce this witness, and as the witness is available here in court, I will allow Mr. Applegate to question her now, while the jury is absent, in order for the state to attempt to establish that it could not have, with due diligence, discovered the evidence to which this witness can testify."

"The state calls Irene Themelis." Everyone in the courtroom peered at the witness, a tall, handsome olive-skinned woman with fierce brows and short, abundant black hair shot through with silver.

The witness was sworn in and settled comfortably in her chair, waiting for the first question. Unlike most people, Caruso thought, she wasn't intimidated in the least by appearing in court.

"Tell us your occupation, please," said Applegate.

"I'm a physician."

"And what is your specialty?"

"I'm a hematologist, a blood specialist. My special area of expertise is blood typing."

Applegate elicited the information that Dr. Themelis had attended Case Western Reserve Medical School, completed a residency at University Hospital in Seattle, was board certified, and had published numerous papers on forensic serology. Presently, she was the director of the Twin Peaks Blood Diagnostic Laboratory.

"Did you call my office this week?"

"Yes, I did."

"Doctor Themelis, could you tell us what prompted you to call?"

"I'd been out of town for a while, and when I returned, one of the girls in the office told me about this trial. She'd been following it in the press. She thought I'd be interested because the victim had been a patient of mine, Benjamin Knapp."

"Did you remember him?"

"I certainly did. Mr. Knapp was one of the few patients who insisted on meeting me personally. He spent about forty-five minutes in my office."

"When you realized that the victim in this case was Mr. Knapp, what did you do?"

"I asked my secretary for press accounts of the trial. When I saw that the evidence turned on blood found at the scene and alleged to be Mr. Knapp's, I realized that we had valuable evidence in our files." She cleared her throat and glanced over at Rebecca. "It was clear to me," she said, "that we might have possession of information that could either save an innocent person or convict a guilty one, so I called you."

The judge cleared his throat. "Under the circumstances, I rule that the prosecution may reopen its case for the presentation of this witness." He motioned to the bailif to return the jury. After they had returned, the judge gave them an avuncular smile. "The prosecution has asked that it be allowed to add something to its case," he explained to them. "This is new evidence that it only recently obtained.

Normally, the state would present its case, followed by the defense responding to it, as I explained at the beginning of the trial.

"So that both the prosecution and the defense might have time to prepare adequately in light of this new development, we will be adjourned until Wednesday morning at ten o'clock."

Caruso lagged at the back of the crowd that followed Rebecca Kendall out onto the courthouse steps. Microphones were thrust in Keegan's face, as he guided his client by the elbow through the crowd.

"What's the new evidence?" demanded one of the reporters.

Keegan ignored them all. Interesting, Caruso thought. Normally he'd seemed pleased to talk to the press.

Rebecca Kendall craned her neck around, as if looking for a way out of the crowd. There wasn't one. When she noticed Caruso, her eyes narrowed and she gave him her customary glare. He gave her a half smile and a little shrug that seemed to say "So what's the big deal?"

She whipped her head back around fast. He put his hands in his pockets and watched her hustled off between Keegan and her fiancé, into their waiting limousine. The car was hemmed in and had to wait to enter traffic.

Even though its windows were tinted, Caruso, through a trick of the light, could see their profiles behind the glass. Keegan was gesturing wildly and shouting. Rebecca Kendall kept shaking her head. Whatever new evidence Applegate had, it was something pretty big.

On Wednesday morning, Applegate again established Dr. Themelis's credentials.

"Your lab administers various types of blood tests, does it not?"

"That's correct."

"Including blood-typing tests?"

"Yes."

"Doctor Themelis, have you met Benjamin Knapp?"

"Yes, I have."

Applegate handed her a large photograph of Benjamin. "Do you recognize this photograph?"

She took it, held it for a while, gave it careful scrutiny, and handed it back. "Yes. It's Benjamin Knapp."

"How did you meet him?"

"He came to our lab and asked to have a sophisticated blood workup. But before he did, he asked for an appointment with me."

"Is that usual?"

"No."

"But you did agree to meet him?"

"He was very insistent. My secretary said he called her several days in a row. So I agreed to see him."

"What did he want?"

"He wanted to know just what kind of tests were available and how accurate they were, how the tests worked and how confidential the results were and so forth. He was very nervous, and I was able to calm him."

"Describe please, Doctor, some of the topics you discussed."

"He wanted to know what kind of tests we performed. I spent some time going over every detail of the DNA test, how we administer the lab, how records are kept and so forth. When I was able to assure him that an opposing party in a lawsuit wouldn't be able to waltz in and grab his records, and that we were very careful with them and kept them under lock and key, he seemed to calm down."

"I imagine you are very careful with your records, aren't you?"

"Of course. The confidentiality and accuracy of medical records is always important, but we do a great deal of forensic work. We must preserve the chain of evidence at all times. My associates and I are often called upon to testify in court. Every sample is la-

197

beled in front of the patient and another witness, every record is initialed and accounted for at every step of the way."

"Did he say why he wanted the test?"

"He said he expected to be named in a paternity suit. I told him he needed a lawyer, not a doctor at that point, but he insisted on having us type his blood."

"And did you do so?"

"Yes."

"Could you explain to the jury, Doctor, just what we can learn from modern blood-typing?"

"Well, originally, we were able to analyze blood and learn the blood type — A, B, AB, or O. Other characteristics of blood could also be analyzed. Now, however, we are able to type blood with a great deal of precision, because we can analyze the DNA itself — the genetic material that makes every human being unique."

"Is this the test you use for paternity testing?"

"There are several tests available. This is more sophisticated than most, but it's the one Mr. Knapp chose."

"I see. Could you explain to us very simply how this test works?"

"Of course," replied Dr. Themelis with a stiff little nod. "First of all, the DNA itself is extracted from the blood in a chemical process. Then we use an enzyme to cut the DNA into particles. We electrofreeze the DNA particles next. They are placed on a gelatinous seaweed solution, and because they are electrically charged, passing a current through them separates them according to size."

Dr. Themelis took a deep breath and plunged on, apparently not noticing or caring that the jury's eyes had glazed over a little. "A nylon membrane is placed over the solution containing the DNA particles, which are wicked up into it. Now various radioactive, phosphorescent probes are applied to the fragments caught on the membrane." She smiled, sounding strangely like someone giving a recipe to a friend. "It's really quite simple. After that, you place X-ray film against the membrane and put it in the freezer at minus seventy degrees — Celsius, of course — for about three days. The result is what we call a DNA print, a series of bands on the X-ray film. It looks like the bar codes used by supermarkets.

"When we compare samples, we place the codes on the same piece of film, and we can see if they match up."

"This is fairly recent technology, isn't it, Doctor?"

"Yes, although we've known that it was

theoretically possible for some time."

"Is there any serious question in the scientific community about the validity of this test?"

"No. It has been accepted as scientifically accurate much more readily than, for instance, fingerprints, or the results of a polygraph examination."

"Is this an example of a test result?" Applegate handed her a file.

She flipped it open coolly, as if she were standing at the end of a hospital bed flipping through a patient's chart. "Yes, it is."

"In fact, Doctor Themelis, that's Benjamin Knapp's file, isn't it?"

"Yes."

"How do you know that?"

"Because of the accompanying patient number, written here in the corner. And the rest of his file is included. I recognize the handwriting and initials of one of my colleagues."

"And this piece of X-ray film is a picture, is it not, of his DNA?"

"Well, that's a simplification, but yes."

"It's as unique as fingerprints."

"At least." The doctor permitted herself a small smile. "I'm not a fingerprint expert, but I do know that fingerprints are not genetically based, so I would assume that the likelihood that two individuals would have identical fingerprints is larger than that two individuals would have identical DNA genetic codes."

Applegate frowned. "Let me make sure I understand you perfectly, Doctor Themelis. You're saying that fingerprints, which I'm sure most of us consider a surefire means of identification, are less accurate than DNA typing?"

"That's right."

"How many samples could result in a pattern identical to this?"

"One."

"You mean there is no chance that someone else has the same genetic code?"

"Aside from a case of identical twins, no other living creature has that genetic code in its blood." The doctor paused. "I can go further than that. No creature that has ever lived has had that pattern."

"Did you receive, Doctor, two samples of blood from Mr. Trivedi, the forensic serologist for the state?"

"Yes, I did."

"And were those samples labeled with the location where they were found?"

"Yes, they were. Sample A came from the mattress at a house at 2667 Carlmont Circle in Oakland, the residence of Benjamin Knapp. Sample B came from the rug in the trunk of a Honda Civic belonging to Rebecca Kendall."

Dr. Themelis was consulting a file now, peering through half-moon glasses she held in place with her forefinger as she bent over.

"And did you subject those two samples to the same test you used on Benjamin Knapp's blood?"

"I did."

"And did you compare them with the results of the test on Benjamin Knapp's blood?"

"I did."

"And what did you discover?"

"That the samples were all from the same person."

Applegate held up a piece of X-ray film with dark stripes on its surface. "This is the DNA print of that test, isn't it?"

The witness glanced at the label in the corner. "Yes, it is."

"And this is the DNA print from Benjamin Knapp's file, isn't it?"

The witness identified it. Applegate put the two cellophane oblongs together and held them up to the light. "They're identical, aren't they?" he said.

"Yes, they are," said the doctor, looking a little irked at this graphic demonstration, perhaps because she'd just told the court that the samples matched.

Applegate introduced both films into evidence.

"The blood from that mattress in the house at 2667 Carlmont Circle and the blood from the trunk of Rebecca Kendall's car and the blood that was extracted from Benjamin Knapp at your clinic are all from the same person? And that person is Benjamin Knapp?"

"There is no other explanation," said Dr. Themelis calmly, but with a trace of impatience.

19

Rebecca, Philip, and Keegan sat in Keegan's Victorian parlor. It had been an hour since Rebecca had heard Dr. Themelis's testimony, and she had barely spoken since. She was shaking and bending over at the waist in her chair, rocking backward and forward. Her body was full of terror, but even now, even when fear seemed to have completely taken her over, she was able to measure her fear. She felt almost as frightened as she had when Benjamin forced her to walk on that beach. But this present fear had a slightly different character. Now there was a horrible bleak sense of hopelessness.

Philip spoke first, glancing nervously at Rebecca, who knew she must look like a mad-woman, rocking back and forth, but finding herself unable to stop. He addressed Keegan. "What does this new testimony mean?" he demanded. "It means it's all over, doesn't it? You can't get her off now, can you?"

Keegan glanced over at Rebecca. "We can

still change our plea."

Rebecca sat upright and grabbed the arms of her chair. "No!" she shouted. The rocking stopped, and she managed to sit very still and straight. "I didn't do it. I'm not going to plead guilty."

"Christ, Rebecca, do what the man says," said Philip. He got up, thrust his hands in his pockets, and walked restlessly over to the bay window hung with flouncy shirred curtains.

"I'm not going to," she said. "You wouldn't want me to lie, would you?"

"I can't put up with much more of this," said Philip.

Keegan sat quietly and watched him pace. Rebecca turned in her chair toward him. "Well you don't have to," she said. "You can always walk away. But I can't. I'm trapped."

"Don't tempt me," he said bitterly.

"I didn't mean that I thought you would abandon me," she said. "You've been wonderful. You really have."

"Well, things are a little different now, aren't they?" said Philip. "I've been loyal and steadfast, but there comes a point when I begin to feel used."

"Used?"

"Oh come on, Rebecca, do you think it's easy to pretend I think everything's all right when it isn't? I've been hanging in there until now, but after today — "

"You mean you think I did it?" She really hadn't considered that possibility before. How stupid she had been. Of course he thought she had killed Benjamin. Keegan did. Probably everyone did. Maybe she had killed him and blanked it all out somehow. It was possible. But wouldn't she know? Wouldn't there be some dreamlike memory of the horror of it? There'd been so much blood.

"Well how the hell did his blood get in the trunk of your car?" asked Philip.

"I don't know," she said. "I can't possibly imagine."

He sighed and turned to Keegan. "I'd like to get out of here right now," he said. "I'd like to go to my office and spend an afternoon at work and pretend none of this ever happened."

Keegan eyed him coldly. "If you walk now, she's dead," he said. "I told you how important it was that you be in court with her every day."

"I've done everything you asked," said Philip, flinging out his arm. "Everything. I've been in court every day. I've neglected my business. I've seen myself on the goddamn news every night, and I'm afraid I come across like a fool."

"So?" said Keegan. "You love her, don't

206

you? You don't mind coming across like a fool it if means saving her, do you?"

Rebecca rose. "You can go any time. I don't expect anything from you. I thought I could. I don't know why."

His face crumpled up a little and he looked at her. "I wanted it to work. I really did. And then, even though I wondered, I wanted to hang in until the end of the trial. Then I thought we could see if it could be put together somehow."

Keegan rose. "We don't have time for this crap right now," he said firmly. "You can sort out the nuances of your goddamned relationship later. On your own time.

"Right now, we've got to decide on an approach to take. I did what I could with that bitch from the lab, but she was very credible. We've got to come up with an explanation for that blood in your car, Rebecca, or change our plea."

"But I'm not guilty." Rebecca sat down again.

Keegan walked over to her, then sat down next to her. He took her hands between his. "Listen to me," he said. "You're making me lose this case. The evidence is overwhelming.

"All you've got going for you right now is Benjamin Knapp and the kind of person he was. I can use that, his terrorizing you all those years. But I can't use it if you stick with a plea of innocent.

"I can get you off with practically no sentence or a suspended sentence if you let me. This is what I do best. I can have that jury in tears in no time. But you won't let me.

"Rebecca, I want you to trust me. You're in no shape to make this kind of decision. Let me decide for you. I'll help you. I'll save you. Just trust me."

She stared at his face, just inches from hers, then felt a surge of relief as tears welled up in her eyes and slid down her cheeks. Her face contorted with the spasm of a sob, then she collapsed against his shoulder and wept, clutching his lapels, burying her face in his shirt.

Philip came and touched her shoulder. "Rebecca," he said softly.

She pulled herself from Trevor Keegan's shirt and turned, blotchy with tears and mascara, to look at Philip. "Go, damn you," she said through a sob. "I don't want you around if you don't love me. I don't want you around just so you can look like a good guy, and so I look like a clinging, helpless woman."

"All right, Rebecca," he said. "I'm going."

"Don't forget," said Keegan, as he left the room. "You're my next witness. See you in court tomorrow morning."

"You can forget that," said Philip heatedly. "I just want out."

"I thought something like this just might happen," said Keegan smoothly. "It's always wise to be prepared." He went over to a telephone sitting on a small marble-topped table, picked up the receiver, and pressed a button.

"Louise?" he said into the instrument. "There's a subpoena for Mr. Patterson in the top left-hand drawer of my desk. See that he gets it on his way out, will you? Thanks, dear."

After Philip had left, Rebecca tried to pull herself together. Sniffing, she burrowed in her purse for her compact, and surveyed the damage.

"I'm sorry I fell apart like that," she said, rubbing at the streaks of mascara on her face.

"I'm surprised you didn't do it sooner." He took a starched linen handkerchief out of his breast pocket and handed it to her. "You've been too brave too long. You've been taking this all on your own shoulders."

"There was Philip," she said.

"He's gone now, Rebecca. I want you to rely on me now." He came and sat next to her.

"You'll want me to plead guilty," she said. "I won't do it."

He surveyed her face, then lifted a wet strand of hair from her forehead and brushed it back. "I won't ask you that, Rebecca. I promise. Just trust me from now on. I think there may be a way. I want you to let me proceed as I see fit. You've been through too much. You mustn't be burdened with details now. I want you to rest and leave this all to me."

Rebecca fought the urge to collapse on his chest once more. She pulled away, handed back the handkerchief, and replaced the compact in her purse. Then she pulled off the emerald engagement ring Philip had given her. Keegan smiled. "That's all right for now," he said, "but I want that on your hand in court tomorrow."

20

Caruso had wanted to leave the courtroom during Keegan's cross-examination of Dr. Themelis. He'd been so startled by the testimony of the prosecution's surprise witness, and by his own reaction to it, that the defense attorney's questioning seemed anticlimactic — even rather pathetic. But he found himself unable to leave.

Keegan had tried to confuse the jury with the technical aspects of the evidence, but Dr. Themelis, unsmiling and occasionally impatient, had repeated herself over and over again in straightforward, simple terms so that no one but a moron could have been confused. Keegan tried to establish the possibility that someone, even the victim himself, could have somehow tampered with samples and records, changing labels and switching the DNA prints, but Dr. Themelis calmly denied that such a possibility existed, and described her clinic's procedures in exhausting detail.

There wasn't much left but to question the

witness's credentials and personal integrity. That would have been disastrous with a witness as self-possessed, confident and slightly supercilious as Irene Themelis.

Caruso had left the courtroom embarrassed for Keegan. He also found himself angry with Rebecca Kendall. Why did she have to lie? They'd got her. Cold. She just looked like an idiot now. She'd screwed it all up. Whatever had happened, it would have been better if she hadn't left the scene and ditched the body; hadn't lied and kept on lying.

Caruso told himself he wouldn't come back. There was a lot of business waiting to be nailed down out there, and none of it was coming his way while he sat in court. Besides, now that he knew she was guilty, what was the point? There was no surprise ending. He guessed he'd been hoping for one.

But he did come back. He came back to see what Keegan was going to do for his client. Maybe she'd change her plea. He wanted her to stop lying.

Michael Caruso observed Philip Patterson carefully as he took the stand. His hair was perfectly parted and combed, his gray suit hung beautifully, his tie was immaculately knotted. But Philip Patterson looked, thought Caruso, very unhappy to be where he was. He'd rather expected him to be overeager. He

212

remembered Philip in his monogramed bathrobe that morning in Rebecca's apartment. He had seemed to be trying to take charge then, to protect her.

It hadn't worked. She'd just let the police into her apartment, let them search her home and her vehicle. How could she have been so passive after having violently killed a man and carted off his body? How could she have been so stupid?

Caruso was as vexed as he'd been when he first met Rebecca. Vexed because he still didn't understand. He prided himself on his ability to size up human behavior. Even madness, he knew, repeated itself in depressingly familiar patterns. Rebecca Kendall, however, defied understanding.

Caruso glanced over at her. He was surprised. She wasn't giving her fiancé an encouraging, grateful smile. In fact, she wasn't looking at him at all. She was very pale, with violet circles under her eyes. It wasn't surprising after yesterday's damaging testimony.

Keegan, however, looked his glossy, sleek, confident self, and almost as if he relished the task ahead. "Mr. Patterson," he began. "In January of this year, you became engaged to Rebecca Kendall, did you not?"

"Yes." It hadn't been Caruso's imagination.

Patterson looked clearly unhappy on the stand. Why?

"And in February, some of your friends gave a party for you and Miss Kendall. Isn't that right?"

"Yes."

"Do you remember that evening?"

"Yes." He glanced over at her. "I was very happy," he said with a little half smile.

Caruso followed his gaze. Rebecca Kendall was looking down at her folded hands on the table in front of her. She could have been praying.

"During the party, did you receive a telegram?"

"Yes, I did."

"Is this that telegram?" Keegan waved a document at Patterson, who removed a pair of tortoiseshell glasses from his inside coat pocket and looked at it.

"Yes, it is."

Keegan had Patterson read Benjamin Knapp's telegram. It had the same frantic tone as all the letters that had already been read into the record. Patterson read it in his pleasant, cultivated voice, as if it were the correspondence of a perfectly sane individual.

"Did you show this telegram to Miss Kendall?"

"Yes, I did."

"And what was her reaction?"

"She was very agitated. She told me that Benjamin Knapp had been harassing her for years."

"You'd never heard about him before?"

"No."

"What was your reaction when you learned about him?"

"It was quite a shock. I couldn't believe my fiancée hadn't confided in me about him."

"Were you angry when you heard her story of years of harassment?"

Applegate looked as if he were about to rise and object, but he frowned and stayed where he was. "Well, to tell you the truth, at first it was hard to believe," said Philip. "But, yes, I was angry."

"You were indignant on behalf of your fiancée?"

Philip Patterson looked slightly confused. "No, that's not what I meant. I was angry with her for not telling me."

"Naturally, you wanted to know about any threat to her."

"Well, yes."

Keegan's voice took on a more forceful tone. "And you wanted to know about any potential threat or embarrassment to yourself, didn't you?"

Applegate, who'd been squirming a little

during this testimony, rose. "Your Honor, I object. Counsel is leading the witness."

Keegan turned on him and looked extraordinarily pleased with himself. "But I'm entitled to ask a leading question of an adverse witness," he said.

Applegate looked stunned.

"Mr. Patterson is indeed an adverse witness," continued Keegan smoothly, "testifying here reluctantly and under subpoena."

The judge asked the witness if this were so. Patterson nodded and looked embarrassed.

"I'll repeat my question," said Keegan. "Isn't it true that you found your situation — being engaged to a woman who was being harassed by a persistent man — rather embarrassing, maybe even frightening?"

"Naturally, my first thought was for Rebecca's safety."

"What was your second thought, Mr. Patterson?"

"Well, the way Rebecca described this guy, he sounded really deranged. Like he'd be following us around, harassing us forever."

"That didn't fit in with the kind of life you'd planned, did it?"

"Of course not." Philip Patterson frowned.

"In fact, Mr. Patterson, you expected perfection in your married life, didn't you?"

"Well, doesn't everyone?" he said, looking

bemused. Caruso glanced over at the jury. A couple of middle-aged women were exchanging smirks. "I mean, I hoped for the kind of success in marriage that I'd had in other areas of my life."

Keegan let that hang there for a few seconds, then continued.

"So your life so far has been perfect. How fortunate for you, Mr. Patterson. You haven't had any real problems in your life."

"None that I couldn't overcome," said Philip.

"So you have had obstacles in life, but you've handled them all."

"Most of the major ones," replied Patterson, trying to sound confident but looking somehow wary.

Caruso smiled. Patterson was coming off like a pompous jerk. The kind of stuff he was dishing out might have gone over well at a job interview, but it sounded ridiculous coming from the witness stand.

"Well, we can all envy you, I'm sure," said Keegan. "How nice it must be to get used to perfection. In fact, in a speech you made at the engagement party your friends gave, you referred to your hopes for perfection in your married life, didn't you?"

"I don't know. I may have."

Keegan glanced down at a card in his hand.

"Didn't you say, after you and Miss Kendall were toasted, 'I waited a long time to get married. I wanted it to be perfect, and with Rebecca at my side, I know it will be'? Does that sound familiar?"

"Yes, something like that."

"And did you add, 'She's the first woman I've met who's beautiful, intelligent, and doesn't have a lot of problems'?"

"Yes, but I was just joking."

"You thought, then, that Miss Kendall was perfect."

"Perfect for me, yes."

"But later that night, after Miss Kendall explained to you about Benjamin Knapp, it occurred to you that Miss Kendall wasn't perfect. She came with some excess baggage, didn't she? Benjamin Knapp."

"I think she should have told me before," said Philip Patterson stubbornly.

"Why do you think she kept this knowledge from you?"

"I guess she didn't want to scare me off," he said.

"I see. And you would have been scared, had you known about Benjamin Knapp?"

Patterson looked insulted. "Not scared. But certainly irritated."

"What did you do when you were threatened by Benjamin Knapp in that telegram?"

"What could I do? Nothing."

"Did you get any further communication from him?"

"He tried to call me at work, but my secretary was instructed not to put those calls through."

"And was this a source of embarrassment to you?"

"Well, yes. The guy was nuts. I didn't want him bothering me at the office."

"You never spoke to him personally? You never told him to back off?"

"No."

"But you did complain to your fiancée, didn't you?"

"I told her about the calls. I told her I was unhappy about them."

"At some point were you aware that Rebecca Kendall was trying to get an injunction against him to keep him away from you?"

"No. She never told me she was doing that."

"So you were upset about Benjamin Knapp. You were annoyed that Rebecca hadn't told you about him. You complained to her about him, and you were unaware she was doing anything about the problem. Is that correct?"

"Yes."

"Did it occur to you, Mr. Patterson, to

219

tackle the problem yourself?"

"Not really."

"It didn't occur to you to meet with Knapp? Tell him to leave you alone?"

"No."

"Would you describe yourself, Mr. Patterson, as an aggressive man?"

"Reasonably so." His tone was decisive, but his expression betrayed confusion, Caruso thought. He was wondering what Keegan was getting at. A glance at Applegate confirmed that he too was in the dark.

"Did you recently write an article for your company's magazine?"

Philip reddened a little.

"Yes."

"What was the title of that article?"

" 'Honing the Killer Instinct,' " said Philip, with a little smile.

"I imagine then, that in business, you are indeed an aggressive man."

"No question about it," said Philip. He seemed more confident when the subject turned to business.

"In fact, you believe that developing a killer instinct is a good thing. You've even taken it upon yourself to help others become more aggressive."

"People who work for me. Yes."

"Yet, when Benjamin Knapp writes you an

abusive telegram and calls you at the office, you don't challenge him. In fact, you don't even take his calls, do you?"

"No."

"The woman you love is worried and upset and you don't challenge Mr. Knapp?"

"No."

"You never decided to do something about the situation?"

"No. I thought Rebecca could handle it."

"You thought Rebecca could handle it? To your knowledge, had she been able to handle it over the many years Benjamin Knapp had been harassing her?"

"No."

"But you chose to do nothing?"

Applegate got to his feet. "Objection. Counsel is badgering this witness."

"Sustained."

"Would you have us believe that you never attempted to confront Benjamin Knapp?"

"That's right." Caruso was leaning forward now.

"You never went to his home?"

"Never."

"Mr. Patterson, what kind of a car do you drive?"

Now Philip looked a little frightened. "A Saab 900 Turbo."

"That's a model without a trunk, correct?"

"There's a third door that opens — a hatch-back-type thing."

"With glass in the window. So that if you carry anything in that space — the space that would normally be trunk space — your cargo is visible. Isn't that right?"

"That's right."

"If you were carryng something you didn't want anyone to see, you'd have to use another car, wouldn't you?"

Applegate leaped to his feet. "Objection. A hypothetical question."

"Sustained."

"Have you ever borrowed Rebecca Kendall's car?"

"Yes. When my car was in the shop. She's borrowed mine too."

"Do you have a key to Miss Kendall's apartment?"

"Yes." Patterson was very pale now.

"To your knowledge, does she have an extra car key?"

"Yes."

"Do you know where it's kept?"

"In her desk drawer."

"What would have prevented you from borrowing her car, unbeknownst to her, if you wanted to?"

"There'd be no reason to."

"But you could have, isn't that correct?"

"I could have. But I didn't."

"We've heard testimony that Rebecca Kendall was harassed by Benjamin Knapp for fifteen years. In all that time, no harm came to him. But as soon as he started to harass you, he was murdered."

"Objection. He's making a speech."

"Sustained."

"Do you expect us to believe she took it upon herself to kill him after all these years?" Keegan seemed agitated.

"Yes." Philip was practically shouting.

Rebecca gasped, and the eyes of the courtroom turned to her.

All feeling gone from his voice, Keegan asked silkily, "So you believe your fiancée killed Benjamin Knapp?"

"I don't know what to believe."

"You've been sitting with her in court every day. Did you ever tell her what you thought?"

"No. I couldn't. I didn't know what to think."

"Can you think of anyone besides yourself who could have had access to Rebecca Kendall's vehicle without her knowledge?"

"No."

"So if Rebecca Kendall didn't use her car to transport Benjamin Knapp's body, you must have. Isn't that correct?"

"But I didn't."

"Answer the question, please."

"Rebecca must have done it."

"So you believe Rebecca did murder Benjamin Knapp?"

He bent his head down. "Yes," he murmured.

"Are you going to marry her?" demanded Keegan.

"No. Our engagement is broken."

"Were you engaged yesterday?"

"Yes, but . . . "

"You were willing to marry a killer yesterday, but not today?"

"I wasn't sure until yesterday that she killed him."

"Or was it that you weren't sure until you yourself were in jeopardy?" Without waiting for an answer, Keegan barreled on. "I submit to you, Mr. Patterson, that you killed Benjamin Knapp, because you didn't want him harassing you and your perfect wife in your perfect marriage. And, when the trail led to your fiancée, you said nothing. When proof was offered that the corpse had been in the trunk of her car, you abandoned your fiancée, rather than admit the truth. You killed Benjamin Knapp."

Keegan's resonant voice had increased smoothly in volume until it had drowned out everything else in the courtroom — Applegate shouting objections, the judge banging his gavel.

Finally all was silent. Keegan's voice was lower now and laced with evident disgust. "No further questions," he said.

At the defense table, Rebecca Kendall was weeping silently. Keegan sat down beside her. "You can take off that ring now," he said.

She turned to him and blinked hard a few times, then she took off the ring and handed it to him. The jury watched in apparent fascination.

Applegate claimed their attention with some throat clearing as he rose to cross-examine Philip.

"I have two questions for you, Mr. Patterson," he said. "They're very simple questions. A simple yes or no will do for an answer. First of all, did you kill Benjamin Knapp?"

"No."

"Do you believe Rebecca Kendall killed Benjamin Knapp?"

"Yes."

"Thank you, Mr. Patterson. No further questions."

Trevor Keegan waived redirect examination, and Philip left the stand and walked out of the courtroom without turning around.

Rebecca leaned over to Trevor Keegan. "I can't do it," she said. "I can't go on the stand."

"Don't worry about it," he said, patting her hand. He stood up. "Your Honor, the defense rests."

21

The blue suit Applegate wore for his summing-up made him look young. It emphasized his fair complexion and golden hair. He approached the jury calmly and confidently, and spoke in measured tones.

"What we have here, ladies and gentlemen, is a sad but simple story. When these two people met, many years ago, they were young, barely out of adolescence. Most of us can remember what a difficult and confusing time that can be. So it was for Benjamin Knapp and Rebecca Kendall.

"I won't go into that relationship here. It was a complex one, and full of strong feeling. At least on the part of Rebecca Kendall. We've heard testimony that she hated Benjamin Knapp and that she wished harm to come to him. She even talked about harming him herself. Her lawyer, Miss Casaretti, has told us how she kept after him legally for years.

"Yet, there's never been a shred of proof

that Benjamin Knapp did all the things Miss Kendall said he did. She had her day in court many years ago, when she brought charges against him. You remember what the judge at that trial said? She didn't have a case.

"But even if Mr. Knapp did harass Miss Kendall, even if what she has charged him with is true — and a court has already thrown out those charges — no one would be justified in taking the law into her own hands." Applegate's voice grew solemn.

"Miss Kendall was never really threatened by the victim in this case. If he was guilty of anything, it was in loving her. If he made a mistake, it was in thinking she was the girl for him. But persistent courtship — caring too much — that's not grounds for murder.

"Sitting here in court, I haven't seen anything that proves Benjamin Knapp was the monster the defense would have you believe him to be. I haven't seen any documents that can actually be proven to have originated with Mr. Knapp. I haven't seen one letter with a signature. A telegram? Anyone can send a telegram."

Applegate took hold of the rail and leaned forward. "Mr. Knapp is not here to tell us his side of the story. He doesn't have that opportunity. Mr. Knapp is dead.

"We know Mr. Knapp is dead because six

pints of his blood were found soaking his mattress." Applegate's voice rose slightly and took on a slight tremor of emotion. "You heard Doctor Trivedi tell us that no one could possibly lose that much blood and live. And you've heard Doctor Themelis explain that that blood belonged, beyond a shadow of a doubt, to Benjamin Knapp.

"We don't know exactly what happened to Mr. Knapp. I'd like to be able to stand here and tell you every detail of this crime, but I can't. There's a lot we don't know." His voice grew slightly sarcastic. "In a murder of this type, there is inevitably a lot we don't know, because murderers don't always tell us what we want to know.

"In this case, we don't know where Benjamin's body was hidden. His mother can't give him a proper burial. All she's been left is evidence that proves he died a violent death.

"Ironically, we know something about his death simply because his body is gone. We know this was no accident. We know this wasn't suicide. We know this was murder. Benjamin Knapp's killer moved that body in a futile attempt to cover up a crime.

"And what else do we know? We know that someone killed Benjamin Knapp, and that Rebecca Kendall hated him and talked about harming him. Those two facts are interesting, but they don't prove a thing. If that's all the state of California had to go on, we wouldn't be here today.

"We're here today because we have a link, a physical link, between killer and victim." Applegate emphasized the point with his fist against his palm. "Benjamin Knapp's blood was found in the trunk of Rebecca Kendall's car. It doesn't take much imagination to see that man's body stuffed in her car, dumped somewhere by a woman who allowed her anger and hate and desire for revenge to consume her.

"And we know that was Benjamin's blood. Doctor Themelis's testimony was very decisive. Thank God for modern blood-typing techniques that make it a lot tougher for a killer to hide the evidence of a horrible crime." Applegate seemed highly indignant now, and he withdrew from the rail and bowed his head, as if gathering his composure. He began again in a quieter voice.

"Now you may look at the defendant in this case and say to yourselves: 'She doesn't look like a killer.' No, she doesn't look like a killer. I've met many killers who didn't. And there's a very good reason for that. Killers aren't a breed apart. They aren't always crazed or wild or out of control." He flapped his arms around.

"They're people just like you and me, who allowed themselves to go over the line. Who allowed feelings of revenge and resentment to consume them. Who chose killing over more reasonable means of settling scores. People for whom hate is stronger than mercy.

"You all know your duty. Your duty is to examine the facts of this case, and to decide whether or not Miss Kendall did in fact kill Benjamin Knapp. And I contend that, based on the facts of this case, no one but Miss Kendall could have, would have, killed Benjamin Knapp.

"Mr. Keegan would have you believe that someone else killed him. Note carefully when this theory was first advanced. It was after Doctor Themelis conscientiously came forward with proof that Benjamin Knapp's body had been carted off in Rebecca Kendall's car. Then, all of a sudden, Mr. Keegan turns on Miss Kendall's fiancé, Mr. Patterson, a man who, it appears, had his doubts about his bride-to-be and her innocence, but who, out of loyalty and decency, had stuck by her during this trial.

"And what's his reward for that kind of loyalty? In the middle of the trial, Mr. Keegan turns on him and accuses him of the crime! Well, I don't think you're going to believe that for a moment. Mr. Patterson didn't hate

Benjamin Knapp. He didn't spend years huddled in conference with Angela Casaretti, thinking up ways to get Benjamin Knapp. He didn't go to Mr. Caruso's office and ask him to find Benjamin Knapp. He didn't tell Mr. Caruso that if he killed Benjamin Knapp, any jury would let him off.

"That's what Rebecca Kendall did. She told Mr. Caruso that she could get away with murder. She thought you'd let her off. I think the arrogance of that point of view is matched only by the arrogance of murder. That's what murder is, ladies and gentlemen — the supreme act of arrogance. A murderer thinks he — or in this case, she — is allowed to decide who lives or dies.

"She thought you'd let her off. She thought she could get away with murder. I think she underestimated you I've worked with enough juries to know what a careful, professional job they do. It's not up to me or the judge or anyone else to decide whether Rebecca Kendall should be held accountable for her acts. It's up to you. I trust you to do the right thing and render a verdict of guilty in this case."

Keegan shuffled papers while Applegate walked back to the prosecution table, then he fussed a little longer after that, so the members of the jury, when he finally came to address them, were eager for him to start.

While Applegate's summation had been generally businesslike, with just glimmers of stronger emotion, Keegan's demeanor was that of a man who is trying to be businesslike, but who is unable to completely conceal his strong feeling.

"You know, ladies and gentlemen," he began, "one thing we lawyers learn about summing up is that it's always a good idea to come right out and state your weaknesses before the other fellow does. That's what Mr. Applegate just did. He said to you, 'There's a lot we don't know.'

"Well, he sure got that part right. Let's talk about what we don't know. First of all, we don't know when Benjamin Knapp died. If we did know, then perhaps my client would have been able to provide an alibi. But no, all we have is the wide parameters — the days between Mr. Knapp's last appearance at work and Mr. Caruso's discovering the scene.

"Not only do we not know when an attack on Mr. Knapp took place, we know nothing about the nature of that attack. We don't know how Mr. Knapp was killed. Was he stabbed, shot? No one knows." He put his hands in his pockets and paced a little, as if thinking out loud.

"And we don't know what happened to the body. It's never been found.

"I think the prosecution in this case is asking you to take a lot on faith. They've come up with one salient fact. Just one. They've found Benjamin Knapp's blood in carpeting that came from Rebecca Kendall's car.

"But have they made it crystal clear to you how it got there? Think about it for a minute. Think about what the prosecution hasn't brought into court. Have they brought in any witnesses? Anyone who saw Rebecca Kendall anywhere near Benjamin Knapp's home? Anyone who saw a car like hers in his neighborhood? Have they brought in any blood-stained clothes? Have they brought in a weapon? No! They haven't even named a weapon.

"What about evidence of Rebecca Kendall's having been at that house? Is there any? The prosecution didn't tell us about it. Fingerprints? Fibers? They would have told us about additional physical evidence if they could have.

"All they've done is link that crime scene to her car. They haven't linked that scene to her. And there's a big difference between a car and a person. Rebecca Kendall wasn't guarding her car all the time. She didn't know what grisly cargo might have been carried in that trunk.

"How do we know she didn't know?" Keegan's voice was growing in volume. He seemed to become slightly agitated. "We know because she made no attempt to keep the police away from her car. They asked her if they could look at it. 'Sure!' she said. Why? Because she had nothing to hide. Mr. Patterson counseled her to call her lawyer, but she had nothing to hide. She told them to go right ahead and take a look.

"Is this the behavior of a guilty woman? Certainly not. Not unless she was stupid too. And Professor Rebecca Kendall is not stupid!"

"If the prosecution could prove that Rebecca Kendall and her car were never separated, then those bloodstains might mean something. But they haven't proved that. Instead, they've linked one place, Benjamin Knapp's house, with another place, Rebecca Kendall's car. That just isn't enough. The prosecution needs to link up two people — a killer and a victim.

"And let's take a look at the woman they would have you believe was the killer in this equation. Why would Rebecca Kendall kill Benjamin Knapp? The prosecution keeps saying she hated him. That may be, but in all the years Benjamin Knapp harassed Rebecca Kendall, she used legal means to restrain him. Why didn't she kill him before?

"Take a careful look at my client, and tell me if you think she's a killer. The woman is a scholar, a university professor. Her life has been devoted to learning, to logic, to reason, to intellectual endeavor. Is this the kind of person who takes the law into her own hands? Who lashes out and kills?

"Take a look at her. How much do you think she weighs? One hundred and twenty pounds? At the most. The prosecution will have you believe she went to Benjamin Knapp's home, went to the home of a man who'd frightened her badly in the past, over-powered him somehow, and killed him in some brutal manner. Then, they want you to believe she managed to cart his body — the body of a man weighing at least fifty pounds more than she — out to her car, get it up into the trunk, and dispose of it somewhere.

"Let's think about this, ladies and gentlemen. You've heard the history of their relationship. Don't you think that if she really did kill him, she'd have been better served by simply calling the police and saying she did it in self-defense? Here was a man who'd threatened her in the past.

"Let's be logical here. The prosecution would have you believe that after killing this man and going to all the trouble to move and conceal the body, she let the police examine her car without a warrant. Is this the behavior of a guilty woman? Of a clever woman? No, it isn't, and you know it and the prosecution knows it."

He paused, gazed at the jurors' faces for a moment, and continued in a softer voice. "You know, sometimes when defense lawyers are trying a murder case, they mention the possibility that an unknown stranger perpetrated the crime with which their client is charged. It's the only explanation that will exonerate their client and fit the facts.

"Well, this case is different. I'm not suggesting some passing stranger killed Benjamin Knapp. I am saying that Rebecca Kendall wasn't the only person with access to that car, and that in fairness we should examine anyone else who might have used that vehicle for any criminal purpose.

"The person who comes immediately to mind is no mysterious stranger. It is Philip Patterson, until recently Miss Kendall's fiancé. You've seen Mr. Patterson on the stand. He's very smooth. He's very attractive. He's very successful. And," here Keegan held up a warning finger, "he's very ruthless.

"You heard the title of the article he wrote — 'Honing the Killer Instinct.' He is an aggressive man, a man who's used to getting what he wants.

"Mr. Patterson wasn't happy to learn about Benjamin Knapp. He wasn't happy about it at all. Perhaps he went over to confront him. Perhaps one thing led to another. Perhaps Mr. Patterson killed Benjamin Knapp.

"Mr. Patterson has told us that the car he drives is unsuitable for disposing of a body. You can see right into the cargo space. If Philip Patterson wanted to move a corpse he'd have to use something else. Like Miss Kendall's car.

"Whether you believe, as I do, this version of events or you don't, you must decide if you think it is possible. Because, as you well know, you can't convict my client if there is reasonable doubt about her guilt.

"Some of you may have wondered why my client didn't take the stand to tell you her own version of the events. The answer is very simple. My client has no knowledge of the events that led to this trial. She has nothing to add that you need to know to make your decision.

"Rebecca Kendall is a very brave woman. She's been terrorized for years by Benjamin Knapp. We heard how he made her life hell. Then, when it seemed as though happiness were within her grasp, she was betrayed by her fiancé, a man who, in my view, wanted her, but wanted her without Benjamin Knapp. When he had to choose between her freedom and his, he decided he didn't want her that much, and betrayed her.

"Add to this the immense strain of a criminal trial, the stigma of an indictment, the public spectacle this trial has become, and you can imagine how she's suffered. Until recently, my client chose to lead a quiet, scholarly life. She was looking forward to marriage and a family.

"It's all been taken from her most cruelly, and she has borne up under the strain with a dignity I think we can all admire." He turned to her with a small smile. "As far as I'm concerned she's endured enough without having to take the stand and be subjected to the prosecution's hammering.

"These charges are simply not plausible," he said, turning back to the jury. "My client is innocent. I don't believe any jury can find her guilty of murder beyond a reasonable doubt. Rebecca Kendall's been through so much that I hope you, the jury, will say, 'She's suffered enough. Let her go.' " He held up his palms and his face took on a seriousness that bordered on melancholy. "When you render the correct verdict in this case — a verdict of not guilty — you'll be giving Rebecca Kendall the pieces of her life back so she can put them together and begin again."

22

Rebecca, lying on the sofa in her apartment, wanted to get up and take a hot bath, but she was too tired. The jurors had been out all day, and the judge had sent them to a hotel for the night.

She'd had dinner with Keegan. "What do you think?" she'd said across the table in the dimly lit restaurant. "What will they decide?" She tried to keep panic out of her voice. She sounded absurdly calm to herself, as if she were asking about a stranger.

"I think we've got a good chance," he'd said. "I really do. But whatever happens, remember, there's always the appeal. I'd like to get you a new trial. I'd be able to go in with a clear strategy from the beginning."

"I can't believe for a minute that Philip — " She trailed off, unable to come out and say it. Philip couldn't be a monster. A monster like Benjamin, but a different kind. She would have known.

Keegan shrugged. "It really doesn't matter

what you think or what I think. It's what the jurors think."

"I should have testified," she said, biting the corner of her lip.

"We've been over this before," he said. "You weren't up to it — especially after Philip turned on you like that."

"That's not really it, is it?" she said, fixing him with a level gaze. "You weren't trying to spare my feelings. If you'd thought I could have helped you win, you'd have put me on the stand."

"Of course," he said. "I would have."

"Why didn't you?"

He leaned across the table and said firmly: "I wasn't sure what you would say or do. With me or with Applegate. You might have decided it wasn't fair to put Philip in the position we did."

Her eyes widened. "You mean you don't believe for a minute that Philip killed Benjamin?"

Keegan shrugged. "Some people might say that anybody who writes an article about honing the killer instinct probably doesn't have one. You know the man. Do you think he could have killed anybody? It's a plausible theory. It fits the facts."

She suddenly felt sick. "You couldn't have been so cynical as to accuse him — just to save me. That's horrible." She bent her head and covered her eyes with her hand. She tried very hard to maintain control. She didn't want him to see how close she was coming to falling apart. Whatever happened, she didn't want to spend any more time with Keegan than necessary. If only the jury let her go, she wouldn't have to. "Look, the way I saw it," said Keegan vehemently, "you had a choice between Philip and serving a long prison sentence, or walking free and using Philip to get yourself out of a pretty bad spot. If he loved you, he would have been glad to allow suspicion to fall on him long enough to establish reasonable doubt. But he wasn't going to stick around anyway, and you know it."

"Maybe not. But you should have asked me before you did it." She pushed her plate away. "Let's see if they're still out."

When she had learned they were still out and that the judge had sent them to the hotel, she told Keegan she wanted to go home and wait by herself.

"Are you sure you'll be all right?" Keegan had said. "Can't you get a friend to stay with you?"

"I want to be alone," she'd said. "If we lose, I might not get to be alone for a long time."

"Nonsense." He waved his hand impatiently. "The appeal process can take years."

"I want to be alone and do things they don't let you do in prison. Like have a long, hot bath."

At the door of the restaurant, as she got into a cab, she had said to him: "Can you see that Philip gets that ring back?"

Keegan smiled. "You've got some pretty big legal bills. That ring's one of your best assets right now. Don't you think I'd better hold on to it?"

"It's the least I can do for Philip. I want to do the decent thing."

"He probably thinks it would have been decent of you to confess," Keegan had said, closing the taxi door.

Lying down in her darkened apartment, Rebecca reflected bitterly that she'd assumed until very recently that Philip would be with her while she waited for the verdict.

Maybe it was just as well this way.

It occurred to her to simply fall asleep here on the sofa in all her clothes. Getting ready for bed seemed like too much of an effort. It all seemed so hard, and what good did struggling ever do, anyway?

When you were alone, there was no one to know if you fell asleep on the sofa with your clothes on. Maybe alone was better. Why had she thought it could ever be any other way?

She couldn't fall asleep, though. Her whole body was tense. Her mind raced along, thinking of every possibility — prison, freedom, Philip calling on the phone. She had imaginary conversations with him and with Keegan and with the press. She realized she was lying rigidly on the sofa with her hands in fists.

Sighing, she swung her feet to the ground and prepared to take that hot bath. Perhaps it would relax her, make her sleepy. She started the water, then went into the bedroom to undress and get her terrycloth robe. Standing barefoot in her slip, she slid open the mirrored doors and saw her own image replaced with rows of hangers and clothes, and then, coming out from between the clothes, a man's arm.

A scream stuck in her throat, and in an instant, she was seized by the shoulders, turned around, and pushed to the floor. She felt a knee in her back. She twisted and began to scream in earnest, but then he wrapped a hand around her mouth.

She shook her head from side to side to escape the smothering hand, but his fingers were caught in her hair, pulling it hard. Then she felt the needle slide into the flesh of her arm. A second later, she was limp and half conscious. A few seconds after that, she slipped into blackness.

The judge looked over his glasses at Keegan. "Do you know where your client is?" he said.

"Your Honor," said Keegan slowly, "I had several numbers for her, and I was unable to locate her anywhere. My associates are looking for her now. I'm very concerned, as my client is a distraught woman."

"The jury has reached a verdict, and we will hear it without the defendant." The judge gestured to the bailiff to bring the jury back in.

She was aware of the motion first. She was in a vehicle of some kind. Then she opened her eyes. She wanted to scream, but she knew she couldn't. She was half choking. She'd been gagged and from the tautness of her face, she imagined there was tape on her mouth. Her arms were tied behind her, her ankles bound together. She shimmied around a little, pulling her head up so she could see her body. She was wearing jeans and a sweater, and the cord that bound her was thin and white like her mother's old clothesline. It was a methodical, neat job. Her feet were still bare.

She was inside some kind of a van with black-tinted windows, and she was lying on her back on a mattress. Next to her was a wheel well containing a spare tire, and a large duffel bag. There was also her own suitcase, sitting rather primly to one side.

It must have been another twenty miles before the van stopped. Rebecca heard free-way noises outside and then the squeaky noise of the van's doors opening. She wasn't clear-headed and had no plan of any kind, so she lowered her lids and feigned unconsciousness. But she kept them open just enough to see through her lashes.

She wasn't surprised. The strange juxtaposition of her own suitcase, apparently carefully packed for a routine trip and sitting there strangely festive in the back of the van, with her own neatly bound and gagged form, brought only one person to mind.

It was Benjamin, all right. She recognized his face beneath the sandy beard and moustache he was wearing. It was the eyes — those pale blue eyes with their fair lashes — that she identified first.

She lay there as he slid the needle into her arm again, and as his lips pressed against her forehead in a chaste kiss. Before she drifted off, she told herself that when she woke next time, she'd have to make use of her consciousness. She'd have to think and plan.

23

"It's sure interesting to meet you, Michael, after testifying at the same trial and all." Sandra Cunningham crossed her big, curvy legs, and he allowed her to intercept a quick, appreciative glance in their direction. She smiled at him.

It hadn't been hard getting an appointment with her. He hadn't even needed to use his vague story about wanting to pitch his services to the insurance company. She recognized his name, and said she'd be glad to talk to him.

"You weren't allowed to hear my testimony, because you hadn't appeared yet," he said. "I was in court when you testified, though."

"Really?"

"Yes." He smiled. "And I decided I'd better come over and talk to you about Caruso Investigations."

"Oh." She looked bemused and a little pleased. "We're not in the habit of using investigators here in the personnel department."

"I'm sure you're aware of some of the developing trends in the employment area," said Caruso briskly. "Nowadays, with so many people ready to sue at the drop of a hat, it's pretty difficult getting honest assessments of applicants from previous employers."

"That's certainly true," she said.

"In fact," he continued, "we've run across cases where employees stole and embezzled, and employers, for fear of libel suits, refused to give them bad recommendations."

Sandra Cunningham looked suitable disapproving.

"That's where a discreet investigator comes in," he continued. "As you well know, making the wrong hiring decision can be a costly mistake. You can't get rid of people the way you used to."

She nodded. "That's why we are involved in drug testing."

His face lit up. "That reminds me," he said, scooting his chair a little closer to her desk. "You said something in court that surprised me."

"I did? What's that?"

"You said Benjamin Knapp was tested for drugs twice. That struck me as kind of funny."

She looked a little embarrassed. "Well of course these things are confidential — "

"I was personally affected by that case," said Caruso. "I found the crime scene. I'm afraid I've become emotionally involved to an extent. I wish I knew more about Benjamin Knapp." He managed to convey a certain slightly brooding sensitivity, and looked out the window.

"I understand," said Sandra Cunningham sympathetically. "It must have been quite something, finding that house and all that, um, blood."

He nodded, and remained silent.

"We tested him once when he was hired, and then once again because — " she leaned forward — "he was acting kind of strange. Wild mood swings. I mean, he always did his work properly and everything. But some of the clericals didn't like working with him. They said he had a weird look in his eyes. And then someone noticed the needle marks in his arm."

"But he came out clean?"

"Oh, yes."

"Maybe he was moody because of a love affair," said Caruso.

"Do you think so?" said Sandra Cunningham. "He wasn't exactly the type. You know, these computer guys are pretty cut and dried."

"But it came out in court that he was worried about a paternity suit," said Caruso.

Sandra Cunningham giggled. "That's ridiculous," she said.

The next time Rebecca woke, he was crouching next to her. He was smiling. She tried not to look terrified, although, of course, her whole face didn't show — just her eyes above the tape. She blinked hard. Her eyes were burning and her head ached. The muscles in her body protested her immobility.

Benjamin looked remarkably different with a beard and moustache, and he also looked remarkably young. It was as if he had never grown older. There were a few lines around his pale eyes, but his brow was still smooth, and his mouth had a kind of adolescent droop to it when he stopped smiling.

"I'm taking off the tape now, Rebecca," he said. "It'll hurt. I'm sorry. I don't want you to scream, okay?"

She nodded with more weakness than she actually felt. She was determined to remain passive for as long as she could stand it, while she decided what she had to do. She knew that she had to do something. She was alone now — without Philip or Keegan. She had to save herself. She had to work somehow with Benjamin's madness, rather than against it, to save herself.

He was right. It hurt when he pulled off the tape. She cried out in pain, but he couldn't interpret that as a scream, surely. She didn't want him upset.

Next, he held her chin and fished a sodden handkerchief out of her mouth. She coughed for a while.

"I'm sorry it had to be this way," he said. "You're such a stubborn girl."

"You're alive," she said thickly.

He grinned. "That's right. And you and I are the only people in the world who know it."

"But Benjamin — the blood, all that blood."

"I'm very smart," he said. "I planned it all very carefully. Of course, I didn't count on that detective calling the cops. But it worked out all right anyway. Maybe better."

"Tell me what you want," she said wearily.

"You, of course." He looked contemptuous. "That's all I've ever wanted. And now, I've fixed it so you'll see that it's the only way."

Tears began to fill her eyes. "Won't you untie me?"

He looked doubtful. "When you're ready," he said after a moment.

"I'm frightened," she said. It was true. It was also, she thought, what he wanted to hear from her.

He smiled. "I'll take care of you. Hungry?"

"Yes." She wasn't hungry at all. She was sick to her stomach. The drugs, probably, and Benjamin himself — the nearness of him.

"What did you put in my arm, Benjamin?"

"Just a sedative. It slows everything down." He frowned. "If you try and run away, remember, I've got lots more. As much as we may need until you learn."

"Learn what, Benjamin?"

"That you're mine, silly."

If he raped her, she thought, she'd beg for some of that sedative first.

"Where are we going?"

"Home." He stroked her hand, then pulled his away as if he were embarrassed.

"Benjamin, let me go. Please let me go. I'm frightened."

He shook his head. "I've worked too hard to get you. I'm never giving you up. You'll learn it's better this way. It was meant to be."

"Where are we now?"

"We're on the way home, Rebecca."

The finality of his tone filled her eyes with tears. Because she lay on her back, the tears slid down the sides of her face.

"Don't cry," he said, an edge to his voice. "Look, we'll go up the road a little further and I'll stop and get us some hamburgers or something."

"I need to go to the bathroom," she said.

He looked surprised. It was clear he hadn't thought of that. He didn't think she was a human being — just some kind of big doll to play with.

"Okay, okay," he said. "In a little while. Now try and get some rest." He scrambled away, opening the back doors and jumping down onto what sounded like soft earth. There were no freeway sounds now, just the sound of crickets, and the air smelled woodsy. It was night.

"You'll like our home, Rebecca," he said. "It's far away from all our troubles." He slammed the doors, and by the dim glow of the dome light she watched the handle turn.

The van bounced along what felt like an old logging road, and then seemed to join a freeway again.

Benjamin had said "up the road." Did that mean north? Or were they headed into the mountains? Did "up" mean an increase in elevation?

She wished she knew how long they'd been gone. Had the jury come back yet?

Benjamin wouldn't have taken her if Philip had been there. If Keegan hadn't turned on Philip, Philip would have been there. Would he have saved her? Now she knew that Philip hadn't killed Benjamin, but now Philip was gone. If she escaped and made it safely home, would Philip take her back? Would he believe her when she said Benjamin was still alive?

Would she still want Philip? Right now, damn it, she would. It hadn't been her idea to frame him. It had been Keegan's. It wasn't her fault at all. But Philip didn't want any kind of trouble, no matter whose fault it was.

What would have happened if Keegan hadn't blamed Philip? She was pretty sure she would have gone to prison. Would that have been better than this? Yes. There'd have been a library and visiting days. And no Benjamin.

Maybe Keegan had saved her by turning on Philip, but wasn't it ironic that by the same action, Keegan drove away Philip, leaving her alone so Benjamin could get to her?

Would Philip have stopped Benjamin? Keegan had told her Philip didn't care, didn't want to save her. He didn't care enough to try and confuse the jury by blaming himself. But who could love anyone that much? She was too hard to love, and it was because of Benjamin. No one could love her except Benjamin himself.

What made her think Benjamin was anyone's problem but her own? It was weak to have expected some man to save her. She'd tried to count on Philip and then on Keegan, and they hadn't helped. There weren't any fairy-tale princes to come around and kiss her and banish Benjamin's spell.

Later, she wasn't sure how much later, the van stopped. Benjamin came and opened the doors. There was some kind of a light outside, and it hurt her eyes. He knelt beside her and undid the ropes.

"We're at a roadside rest," he explained. "There's no one else here. I'll be waiting for you outside the ladies' room door. You have ten minutes. Then I'll come in and get you. If anyone pulls up, I'll come in with this." He held a syringe in front of her face, so close she could barely focus on it. "I'll sedate you, then carry you out, and tell them you passed out drunk."

She rubbed her wrists with her swollen fingers.

"Don't disappoint me, Rebecca," he added sternly.

"I won't," she heard herself saying.

He had to help her out of the van. Her legs buckled under her and she resisted the urge to try and push him aside while she got her legs working. She didn't want to intimidate him. She wanted him to think she was growing dependent on him. She'd wait for her chance. It had to come sooner or later.

The restroom was cold. Mosquitoes batted against a tiny wire-mesh window high above.

There was only one way out, and Benjamin was standing there. She wanted to take all of her ten minutes. It might be the only time she could be alone for a while. But she didn't want to take more than ten minutes. She didn't want him rushing at her.

At the sink, in front of a stainless steel vandal-proof mirror in which she saw her own haggard, distorted reflection, she found, to her annoyance, only cold water. She'd wanted to run warm water over her wrists where the cord had been.

She felt dirty. She washed her hands in cold water, wanting to clean any place he'd touched her. Then she scrubbed her face hard, using soap that stung her skin.

After hours of sensory deprivation, she was acutely aware of everything around her — the grainy pink institutional soap with its harsh smell, the obscene graffiti in black felt-tip pen, the wet, red tiles beneath her bare feet. Sighing, she dried her hands on paper towels, slowly, carefully, savoring even this simple task because it was one she had chosen to do herself — a free action.

The graffiti gave her an idea. She must leave a message here. On the mirror. But there was nothing to write with. The soap was powdered. She frantically pawed through the trash can, looking for something, anything, an old lipstick maybe.

Instead, she found the *San Francisco Chronicle*. The headline read "Rebecca Kendall Vanishes. Jury Says: Guilty."

"Rebecca!" Benjamin was calling her.

"Coming!" she shouted as she tore off the front page, folded it up, and jammed it into the front pocket of her jeans.

She knew now that she couldn't try to escape. If they hadn't believed her before, they wouldn't now. She had to show them Benjamin. Alive.

24

"I wasn't sure you'd want to have lunch with me." Caruso fiddled with his wineglass. Across from him, in a small Italian restaurant near their building, sat Angela Casaretti.

"I'm not sure why I wanted to talk about Rebecca," she said. "With you, especially."

"This week, two authors have called me about books they're doing on the case, and an agent wanted me to write one myself."

"I got a few of those calls myself."

She looked at him suspiciously. "You aren't writing a book, are you?"

"No," he said. "I wouldn't know how it ends."

"I know how it began," said Angela.

He leaned toward her eagerly. "That's what I wanted to know. I wanted to know how it began. What happened on that beach?"

"Why do you want to know?"

"Because I don't understand it. It doesn't ring true. It doesn't make sense."

"I thought you understood it fine," she

said. "You called the cops and turned her in."

"I told them what I knew. I had to. But now I think there's a lot more I don't know. There has to be."

"He drove her mad," said Angela. "Looking back on it, I wonder why he didn't push her over the edge long before."

"Then why didn't she plead insanity?"

Angela narrowed her eyes and twirled her pasta slowly. "If I'd been representing her, I think that's what I would have advised."

"Did Keegan think he could get her off clean?"

"I really shouldn't speculate." Angela frowned. Then she said slowly, "But after that DNA testimony — "

"There was nothing left but to try and throw Philip to the dogs," finished Caruso.

"Kind of looks like it, doesn't it?" Angela sighed. "It just makes me sick, her bolting like that. There's always an appeal. And it's so unlike her. She's always been so straightforward, ready to take consequences. She must have panicked, but that's not like her either.

"You know, Michael, if she hadn't run away like that I might have been able to believe — " She paused.

"That Philip did do it?"

Angela shook her head. "I wish I thought

259

he did. But I still don't know why you're so interested."

"I'm a detective," he said with a little smile.

"Well the case is closed. The jury decided she did it." She put her hand to her forehead and there was a little tremor in her voice. "I keep thinking I should have been able to help her sooner. But I swear to God I did everything I could for her. I know I did."

"Everything legal," said Caruso. "Somebody should have scared the hell out of Benjamin early on. Physical threat. That's all a guy like that would understand."

"Oh, really?" Angela was sarcastic. "The little lady lawyer and her helpless female client weren't enough. Some macho guy should have threatened to break his legs. Is that the kind of a cop you were?"

"Well, what was the matter with Philip? Why couldn't he look after her better?" Caruso looked angry.

"Oh, sure. Philip was supposed to go over there and kick ass. Listen, women can't wait around for some man to take care of things for them. Those days are over. This isn't the wild West."

"As long as there are bad guys, it'll always be the wild West," he said firmly.

Angela's eyes widened. "So *that's* it. That's why you're so interested. You wish you could have saved her. Thrown her on the back of your horse and ridden off into the sunset. You're in love with her."

"I hardly knew her," he said with a dismissive wave of his hand. "And she wasn't very pleasant the few times we talked. Mostly, I've seen the back of her head in court."

"Rebecca, wherever she is, would get a big laugh out of this," said Angela. "She gets rid of Benjamin, and then someone else claps eyes on her across a crowded room and falls in love with her. Terrific. Maybe she'd better stay where she is."

Caruso bristled for a second, then he allowed his face to relax into a charming smile. "Come on, counselor," he said. "I just want some background. Help me out, will you? I want to understand."

"First you come across like John Wayne, now you're the sensitive Phil Donahue type who just wants to understand. I don't buy it, Michael. I grew up around too many Italian men."

He kept smiling. "Come on, Angela. Give me a break."

She looked at him seriously for a moment and then said, "Okay. I'll tell you how it happened on that beach. When I'm finished, maybe you'll understand why she did it."

"But I'm not completely convinced she did do it," he said.

"Here we are." Benjamin's voice sounded cheerful. He was opening the van doors, and she propped herself into a sitting position and looked eagerly over his shoulder. She saw tall evergreens with rays of sunlight streaming at angles between the branches.

"You'll love it, Rebecca, you really will. When you see what I've prepared for us, you'll realize what a great life we can have together."

She crawled to the doors and slid out. Wherever she was, it had to be better than the back of the van, trapped behind tinted windows. It smelled of the hamburgers and fries they'd eaten the night before. Outside it smelled fresh and even a little damp.

He held her arm tightly. "You can't run now," he said. "There's nowhere to run." Ahead in a clearing she saw a cabin of neatly peeled logs. It was long and narrow, with darkened windows.

"Oh God," she said, panic rising, "please, please let me go. Let me go. Let it end." He had her now, completely. He could do whatever he wanted with her. He would rape her, she was sure of it. The thought of his body and hers joined together sent waves of nausea

262

through her. She began to tremble and wondered if it would be better to die than to submit to Benjamin.

"But it's just beginning," he said indulgently.

"Let me go home," she said, her voice shriller.

"This is home. You'll get used to it."

She tried to shake off his arm, but he held her tighter, and his face changed in an instant from pleasant and slightly foolish to a mask of anger.

"I'm sorry," she said with a whimper, terrified at his sudden change of mood. "It's so hard to get used to this."

The rage vanished as fast as it had appeared. "Everything will be wonderful," he said. "You'll see."

He pulled her toward the cabin and through a large room with a stone fireplace up to a thick door. She saw with horror that there were brackets on either side of the door big enough to hold the two-by-four that stood on end against the wall.

"I know it will take some time to adjust," he said. "I'm willing to be flexible. But someday, Rebecca, I know how grateful you'll be that I went to all this trouble for you."

She lowered her eyes demurely. "Goddamn you," she said to herself. "Goddamn you to hell. As soon as I can, I'll get away, but I'll kill you first if I can. They can send me to prison. I don't care."

Michael Caruso spent a restless weekend. On Sunday, he took a long walk around North Beach. He passed the Church of Saints Peter and Paul as everyone was leaving mass. On an impulse, he went inside and sat in the last pew of the empty church.

He thought for a while, gazing idly at the altar and smelling the waxy smell of the candles he associated with his childhood. He was surprised to find himself saying a prayer for Rebecca Kendall.

Later, he walked past a newsstand and picked up the Sunday paper. As he handed over his change, his eye fell on a bodybuilding magazine. It reminded him of the magazines he'd seen at Benjamin Knapp's house.

He read the title of one of the articles emblazoned across the grotesque image of a grimacing giant. "Blood Doping. How It Works. What It Can Do For You."

Rebecca knew just what Benjamin was doing. He'd kept her in that room for two days. He was counting on the fact that isolation would make her desperate to see another human face. Even his.

264

She'd examined every inch of her room. There was nothing much there. A bed. An empty chest of drawers. She'd unscrewed the knobs to see if they could be turned into a weapon, but the screws that held them in place were tiny.

There was a bathroom with one skimpy towel, a toilet, a sink, a metal shower stall and a bar of soap. There wasn't a mirror. If there had been, she would have been able to see her own face, anyway. It might have been a comfort.

She read and reread the article in the *Chronicle*. It was mostly about her disappearance. Keegan was quoted as saying he feared for her, that she was a distraught woman.

There was less about the verdict, but there was an interview with one of the jurors. It was the woman with sallow skin, juror number ten, the one Keegan hadn't wanted. "We just couldn't buy it that Mr. Patterson did it," the juror said. "If we could have believed that he did, we might have decided differently, but he seemed so normal on the stand. Like a real nice guy. It seemed like he was just getting blamed. And, of course, we never got to hear Rebecca's testimony."

She should have testified, though, even if the verdict had been different, she'd still be here. But people wouldn't look for her as hard. Now she was a fugitive.

She had gone through her suitcase over and over again. There was something comforting about the few possessions that were hers. He'd packed jeans and sweaters, shirts and underwear. There was also a flannel nightgown and a toothbrush. One item, however, she'd removed and put in a bottom drawer, out of sight. It disturbed her too much. It was the dress Philip had helped her buy — the green Audrey Hepburn dress. It had been slashed to ribbons from shoulder to hem.

There was no window in the room, so she didn't know if it was day or night. He'd been bringing trays of food for her. She'd see the door open, then his hands appear around it with the tray, then the door would close, and the two-by-four would fall heavily into place.

She didn't know how much longer she could stand it, but she was determined to wait him out. She knew he wanted her to speak to him when he brought the trays or took them away. She knew he wanted her to pound on the door and beg for him to come.

But she hated him too much. When she cried, she muffled her sobs with a pillow.

On Monday morning, Caruso went to work and made a phone call. He found out the name of the bail bondsman who'd put up Rebecca Kendall's bail. He was pleased to learn it was Ken Chavez, with whom he'd had dealings with before. He called Ken in Oakland.

"Caruso! Hi. How ya doing?"

"Okay, Ken. I understand you put up the bail for Rebecca Kendall."

"That's right. That bitch skipped and I'm out fifty grand minus five. Serves me right for trusting a nice clean-cut college professor. She was a head case, no doubt about it."

"If I find her for you, is there a fee in it?"

"Sure. Be my guest. Usual percentage. You got any ideas where she might be?"

"Maybe," Caruso lied.

"Half the state's looking for her. I wish you luck."

"I'll see what I can do, Ken."

"Maybe you got her over at your place. Not bad-looking. But nuts. And mean too. Remember what happened to that other guy." Ken Chavez laughed, then said, "What the hell am I laughing about? Right now, I'm out forty-five thousand. Shit."

"Listen, Ken, I'll get right on it. Do me a favor, will you? Make me a copy of the fugitive warrant and send it over to my office. The forfeiture of bail notice too."

When Caruso had hung up, he thought about calling Keegan for an appointment, but decided just to show up at his office and ask to see him.

He was going to bring back Rebecca Kendall, he'd decided. But first, he'd have to find her.

25

All alone, Rebecca wondered when it would happen. Could she do it? Could she have sex with him if it would mean her freedom? His guard would be down. Would it be worth it if she could kill him? Or would she rather die first?

The door opened. This time it opened all the way. Benjamin stood there.

"Aren't you lonely?" he said.

"Yes, I am," she replied, trying to stop herself from sobbing or screaming or flying at him and tearing at his foolish face with her fingernails.

"Look, there's nowhere for you to run. Let's sit in the living room for a while and listen to records."

"All right, Benjamin," she said. "I'd like that."

He got behind her and followed her into the main room. There was a fire in the fireplace and some bookshelves and a stereo.

He went over to the stereo and chose a

record. "Later, you can have your own records," he said. "I know you like classical music. But for now, we'll listen to my records."

As he bent over the turntable, she glanced at the fireplace. Was there a poker there? Before she could see, he turned around quickly. "Sit down," he said. "You're making me nervous."

She sat on one of the sofas at the end farthest from him. He sat, to her relief, on the opposite sofa. The sounds of Johnny Mathis singing a love ballad filled the room.

"Benjamin," she said, "tell me how you did it. How you fooled everyone."

"If I tell you," he said solemnly, "and you ever run away, you might tell someone. I'd be in trouble then."

She realized than that he'd had to give up everything himself, whatever kind of life he'd had. "You can't go home either, can you?" she said softly, trying to put some sympathy in her voice.

"This is home," he said. "Would you like some wine?"

"No, thank you."

"I saw you drink wine with Philip." He looked annoyed. "But this can't be our home forever," he continued. "My plan got a little messed up. You see," he smiled triumphantly,

"I had it all figured out. I was going to leave all that blood there, and then I was going to get you. And *then* I was going to tell the police that you did it. Anonymously, of course. I'd tell them about the clinic and my blood workup and the DNA print.

"They would have come to talk to you, but you would have been gone. They would have thought you ran away. And then you would have had to stay with me or be arrested."

She looked over at him and reminded herself once again that he was completely mad. It was a bizarre plot, and there were a lot of ways it would never work. But still, here she was.

"But I was arrested anyway," she said.

He giggled. "I know. I was pretty mad about that at first. That nosy detective went to my house and called the cops. You were arrested before I could get you."

He rose and she pushed herself deeper into the corner of the sofa.

"Are you sure you don't want some wine? I'm going to have a glass."

"All right," she said, not wanting to stop him from talking.

"I thought my plan was ruined there for a while." He went over to the sideboard and poured wine into two glasses. "But it's better this way. I had to wait a long time — until that Philip stopped staying at your house. Which

271

happened to be while the jury was out.

"I had to get you before they came in with a verdict. If they let you off, my plan wouldn't work." He smiled. "They found you guilty, you know."

"I was afraid of that," she said, turning her face away. She didn't want to tell him she'd found the newspaper. He seemed to want total control.

He handed her a glass and went back to his own sofa. "It's really better this way," he said. "Because now if you go back, they'll send you to prison. Now you really have to stay here with me."

"You've been very clever, Benjamin."

He frowned. "You're just saying that to butter me up. You don't care about me. But you will."

"Maybe I will," she said. "It's all so new and strange."

"No, it isn't. I've known you were the girl for me from the very beginning. That day in the library."

She turned her eyes slowly around the room. There was a poker. Could she kill him with it? It didn't look very heavy. Could she get close enough? He'd stop her arm with his. She had to get him off guard.

"We may have to move, though," he said thoughtfully. "I didn't count on your being so

272

famous. Of course, it made it easy for me to find out what you were up to. It was on the news every night. And so was your face. Mine too in that old photograph.

"We'll stay here for a while, then we'll move on. We can go into the high country for the summer and live in a tent. It'll be a wonderful adventure. I know a lot about the woods. I can live off the land.

"After that, we can move to Canada or Mexico. No one will know us there and we can get new identities. We can get married."

"I guess that's what you've always wanted, isn't it?"

"That's right." He nodded happily, then he wagged a finger at her archly. "And I'm not taking no for an answer."

"Oh Benjamin," she said, sighing. "I don't know what to think."

"You don't have to think," he said crossly. "I'm doing the thinking for us from now on. You weren't very good at it, so I had to take over. You weren't sensible about this at all."

She thought about the poker. She'd kiss him, get him all excited, maneuver him around by the fireplace, then — when he was least expecting it — she'd crease his skull with that poker. If only she could get proper leverage. Maybe he'd kill her, but she would have died trying. Right now, it didn't seem like she had much to lose.

"But Benjamin, I don't know if I could love you — in that way," she said with a shy downward glance. That's what he wanted. He wanted her to be childlike, demure, virginal. He had to think everything was his idea.

He rose from his sofa and came toward her. She had to keep the nausea from engulfing her. She swallowed hard and closed her eyes for an instant. He kneeled before her. "Rebecca," he said softly, as Johnny Mathis crooned on, "will you marry me? Say yes."

"But I don't know enough about you. Maybe if we — " She bent down and kissed his cheek. He began to tremble. His hand, shaking and damp, came up to her face and turned it as if he were about to kiss her on the mouth. Then he pushed her away.

"You fucking slut," he whispered, his pale blue eyes gleaming with a strange light. "I know you've slept with Philip. God knows what filthy things you let him do to you. God knows who else you've slept with. You've ruined yourself. I hope you aren't always going to be a cheap whore."

He slapped her hard across the face.

She burst into tears of fear. Even frightened, she thought to herself, "It's good he sees me afraid. He likes me better this way."

He pulled her to her feet and bundled her into her room, slamming the door closed and barricading her in. "I'm sorry," she shouted, leaning against the door and sobbing.

He played both sides of the Johnny Mathis album, and then the house was silent.

The next morning, he came to her door again. This time when he opened the door, she cringed, but he was smiling. "Gee, I'm sorry we had that little spat last night," he said. "But I guess you'll agree you had it coming."

"Whatever you say," she said in a weak little voice. Was she acting? She wasn't sure anymore.

"Listen, Rebecca, we'll get along just fine if we wait to get to know each other better before any of that, um, sex stuff. I'm right, you know. My parents were virgins before they married. It's better that way."

"Yes, I'm sure you're right," she said. "Can I come out now, Benjamin, please?" She had a sudden inspiration. "Can't I make you breakfast?"

"Oh, that would be nice," he said tenderly. He was genuinely pleased with her, she could tell. "But I won't let you run away."

She wiped away a tear. "I won't," she said. "I know how determined you are, Benjamin."

"That's my girl," he said. "I guess I better tell you how I like my eggs. Over easy. But not too hard. The yolks still runny."

"All right," she said. As before, he walked behind her into the kitchen, a room she'd glimpsed last night from the sofa.

It was an old-fashioned kitchen with a big pine table, a wood stove, and a row of cast-iron skillets hanging on hooks above it. Checkered curtains hung at the window over the sink.

She gazed out at freedom from that window with something like intoxication. It had been so long since she'd seen natural light. But she couldn't allow herself to be diverted by daylight.

"Sit down," she said, smiling.

"There's an apron on the hook behind the door," he said. "I thought of everything."

"You certainly did," she said, opening the door and finding an old-fashioned flowered apron there. She slipped it on over her head, then, humming, she arranged eggs, butter, bacon, and utensils. She worked silently while he sat at the table watching her appreciatively. She turned and looked over her shoulder at him a few times.

When she'd found plates and silverware, she set places for both of them. She trembled when it was time to turn the eggs over. She didn't want to break the yolks or get them too hard. She never cooked eggs over easy and she hoped she got it right, just the way he wanted it.

They were perfect. She was sure of it. "You'll like them," she said. "They're just the way you want them." She slipped her hands into oven mitts and carried one skillet with the eggs, the other with the bacon, over to the table. She held down the eggs for him to admire and approve, and when he did, she threw the hot bacon grease from the other skillet into his face. He screamed, clapping his hands over his face. Then she raised the skillet with the eggs high above her. The eggs flew backward as the skillet made an arc toward his head.

The blow knocked him off his chair, and she bent over him as his eyes rolled back in his head. Then she tore off the apron. That flowery thing, like aprons her mother had worn when Rebecca was a little girl, had practically driven her to hysterics. This odd accouterment of some life Benjamin must have seen on old TV shows seemed as bizarre as anything he'd ever done.

26

She had let the small skillet with the bacon fall to the ground with a dull clang. Now she held on to the bigger one, the one that had held the eggs, the one she'd struck him with, and stepped back a few steps, keeping her eyes on him, then she stepped forward again.

She started to raise the skillet one more time and bring it down heavily on his head, but she stopped. She wasn't sure whether he was alive or dead — he didn't look like he was breathing, and only the whites of his eyes showed.

It would be better if Benjamin were alive. Then they'd all see that she hadn't killed him, that he was a liar. If she slammed that skillet down on his head now, would it be murder? Would she be back in court, explaining why she'd really killed him this time? She knew that if she did kill him right now, she'd get immense satisfaction from the act. That feeling, more than anything else, stopped her. To enjoy killing him — wouldn't that make it murder?

She knew she wasn't thinking clearly. Her heart was pounding, and she felt an urge to run out of the cabin and keep running.

But she had to try and think. She had to get the police or somebody, and bring them back here. She wondered how long he'd stay unconscious, and how far away she was from civilization. She'd have to take his van. Dropping the skillet, she backed away from him.

She ran into the living room and looked around. There was a black leather bag on the sofa. She went to it and fell to her knees, pawing through it, looking for keys. There weren't any keys there, but she found something else. One of his syringes. It was full. It must have been the one he'd had ready at the rest stop on the freeway.

She was breathing heavily, and there were tears in her eyes, tears of relief. Sniffing, trembling, she took up the syringe, and wondered if she could inject him. She'd had a cousin who was diabetic. She'd spent one summer with her, and watched her inject herself many times. She was sure she could do it.

She went back into the kitchen reluctantly. What if he came to and leapt at her while she tried to inject him? He looked definitely unconscious, though, in a heap on the floor. If she killed him, she might have to stand trial again. She couldn't bear that. She had to keep him alive.

Frightened, she went over to him, pushed some of the liquid in the syringe out the top, then carefully raised his sleeve up and plunged the tip of the needle into the part of the arm where it seemed nurses and doctors always gave shots.

He didn't flinch when she injected him. That gave her the courage to search his pockets for the van keys. His pockets were all empty. She realized he was still breathing, though it was shallow.

She got out of the kitchen as fast as she could, even though she knew he was definitely out, and began to search for the keys, running through the cabin, throwing out the contents of drawers, even searching under the sofa cushions. If she found the keys, could she drag his body into the van and take him somewhere — to the police? The damned jury had thought she could handle his body, get it into a car, but she wondered whether she in fact could.

When she found herself searching the same places for a second and third time, she realized she was in a state of panic. "I have to get out of here," she told herself. "I have to get out of here right now. Whatever is out there, I can handle it. If I stay here, I'll suffocate from panic."

She had to leave on foot, find help, and bring the police back to the cabin and show them Benjamin. She decided to forget about her suitcase and clothes. She could get her things when she brought the police back here. Or sent them back. She wasn't sure she'd be able to set foot in this place again.

As soon as she ran out the front door and across the clearing she began to laugh hysterically. She ran down the logging road that led to the property, and it wasn't until she'd gone far enough to exhaust herself that she stopped laughing.

The laughter, echoing in her memory, suddenly frightened her. She realized how loud she had sounded in the forest, and how silent everything was around her. She wondered how many miles it was to a real road.

And then what would happen? She'd have to flag down a car. She'd be vulnerable, all by herself. Suddenly she realized she wasn't wearing shoes. In her panic, in her exhilaration, she hadn't even noticed that her feet were getting cut.

If the police found her, would they believe her? Would they listen to her? Or would they just pack her off to jail? They might not consider her a good bail risk any more. She might be in prison during the appeal process, trying to tell them Benjamin was alive. She'd tried to explain to people about Benjamin before, and no one had believed her. Would they believe her now?

She made her way more slowly, grateful that there was a road for her to follow, listening to the sounds of her own feet and of birds above, watching dust rise from the road, illuminated by the light filtered by tree branches. Once she was startled by a deer that fled across the road, its hind legs seeming to go in the opposite direction from its forelegs as it leapt away.

After a while, she had no idea how long, she came to a fork in the road. One way seemed to lead down the hill, toward some kind of a valley. The other appeared to go deeper into the woods. But why would it be here at all unless it led somewhere? There must be another cabin at the end of the road.

The idea of approaching some kind of habitation appealed to her more than flagging down a car on the road. She took the path that led into the forest.

It was hours later, she was sure, that she first saw the column of smoke, clearly from a campfire or a chimney. She'd stopped and rested a couple of times, and the last time she'd been afraid she couldn't get up again, but she was determined to keep going on the energy she knew was false — a rush of adrenaline leading her away from Benjamin. Now it looked as if it was going to pay off.

It had taken hours, but finally Caruso was sitting in Keegan's office, glancing quickly around him at a lot of red velvet and flocked wallpaper. It reminded him of an ice cream parlor or some kind of shopping center steak house with a Gay Nineties theme.

"All right," said Keegan irritably. "You've got fifteen minutes."

Caruso ignored the insult and came straight to the point. "I figured out how Benjamin Knapp could have done it and lived," he began. "I think I could develop some new evidence to get your client off."

Keegan's eyes narrowed. "Wonderful," he said. "And where were you when I needed you?"

"I testified to the facts as I knew them," said Caruso. "Since then I've uncovered a few more facts."

"Oh, really?" Keegan sneered.

"Possibilities, anyway. I'm very worried about Rebecca Kendall," continued Caruso. "She may have been abducted. By Knapp."

"Just what is it you're selling, Mr. Caruso?"

"Look," said Caruso, his voice rising, "you're her attorney. I've got to tell you what

I think might have happened. Could you just listen?"

A very young, ashen-faced secretary came into the room. "A very important call on line three," she said to Keegan.

"I can't take it now," he snapped.

"It's collect."

"Then I certainly don't want to take it," he barked at her, waving her off and turning back to Caruso.

"It's her," said the secretary rather desperately.

Keegan's eyes lit up, and he rose, waving now at Caruso. "Excuse me," he said. "I don't know what this is about, but I'll have to find out, apparently." He followed the young woman out of the room.

"You know exactly what this is about," thought Caruso with grim satisfaction. As soon as Keegan cleared the door, Caruso went over to a small marble-topped table and punched the third button, which was blinking up at him. Then, very slowly, he lifted the receiver.

"Where are you?" Keegan was saying, trying to sound calm. "Tell me exactly where you are."

"North. Near the coast. Between Crescent City and Ukiah. I'm at a place called Bill's Resort. A bunch of cabins on a lake.

Taylor Lake, it's called."

"Do they know who you are?" asked Keegan.

"Not really," she said casually. "There's so much to tell you."

"Is someone standing there?" Keegan asked.

"That's right." Caruso admired the calm she managed to project.

"Stay there," directed Keegan. "Don't move. I'm coming to get you."

"I explained to the people here how I got lost camping," she said. "I didn't know if I should call the police or what. My wallet's gone, of course."

"Don't call the police," said Keegan. "Stay there. I'll be up in a matter of hours. Let me talk to the people there. Then lie low. Don't call anyone else."

"But so much has happened — "

"Don't worry about a thing. I'll take care of everything. We can explain all this to the court. But you have to stay there until I come and get you. You'll be coming back voluntarily, with your attorney. It's the best way. I'll arrange everything."

"I'm so tired," she said, and her voice began to crack.

"Put on the desk clerk or whoever's there," he said firmly. "Then ask them if you can lie

285

down for an hour or so. I'll explain everything."

Caruso was furious. Keegan could have
asked her a lot of questions. He could have
found out what had happened — if Benjamin
were alive.

Another voice came on, a man.

"Hello," said Keegan with smooth charm.
"This is Trevor Keegan down in San Francisco. I'm an attorney representing the family
of the young lady you've got there. I'm coming up to get her right away. Can you give her
a place to rest?"

"I guess that would be all right," said the
voice. "There's no one here right now. Fishing season doesn't start until next week, so all
the cabins are empty."

"Well, believe me, her family will make it
worth your while. She's from a very promi-
nent family, and they're worried about her."

"I guess so." The voice sounded a little
dubious. "Camping alone. Wandering around
the woods. She didn't even have shoes on.
The wife had to give her a pair of tennis
shoes."

"I'm going to take you into my confidence," said Keegan with a kind of breath-
lessness. "This poor young woman has had a
lot of problems. She's been under a psychiatrist's care. The family doesn't want any pub-

licity. Can we ask you to let her wait there for a few hours, without telling anyone else about this?"

"Oh. Well, just what exactly — " The voice trailed off. Obviously Rebecca was standing there, and the man was too shy to ask Keegan just what kind of a nut he had on his hands.

"She just gets confused sometimes. Kind of amnesiac." Keegan was extemporizing a little wildly, Caruso thought. "Her family, I am sure, will show you its appreciation for handling this matter discreetly." He paused, waiting for some kind of a reaction, and then he added, "They're very wealthy people, and they're very concerned."

"We'll fix her up in one of our cabins," said the man.

"How big's this lake of yours?" said Keegan. "Can I get a float plane on it?"

"Oh sure. You'll find us on any map. We're at the northern tip of the lake. Greatest trout fishing in the world," he added.

"Fine, fine," said Keegan. "I know I can count on you, Mr. — "

"Just plain Bill," said the man. "That's all anyone's ever called me. Like the radio show."

"Sure," said Keegan affably. "See you soon, Bill."

After Keegan hung up, Caruso hung up. Then he walked over to a door next to the fireplace in the parlor. He opened it slowly and discovered it was a closet.

In an old house like this, remodeled into offices, it was hard to guess what the floor plan might be. This closet, however, suited his purposes exactly, because it seemed to project into the inner office. He could hear Keegan quite clearly through the wall, especially as Keegan seemed to be bellowing to his associates and secretaries.

"Tell Kevin to go to court for me this afternoon and cover for me in the Griswold matter.

"Then call that air charter service we used before. I need a float plane right away.

"Then get Dr. Greenberg on the phone. I want him to get ready to do a complete psychiatric evaluation right away, as soon as I bring her back. No, I've got a better idea, tell him to get over here right now. He can fly up with me and we can do all that on the plane coming home. And when I get back, I want an affidavit for him to sign and fill in.

"Then call the press — both dailies and all the network affiliates. Tell them we'll have an important announcement in the Kendall case later this evening. I may call in from up there and see if we can get some cameras to meet the plane.

"And will somebody go throw that wop detective out of the meeting room?"

Caruso smiled and stepped back into the parlor. He selected a couple of Trevor Keegan's business cards from an ornate little card holder on a low table, and sat down, assuming an impatient air.

The young secretary who'd told Keegan he had a call came in. Caruso stood up. "Tell your boss I'm leaving," he said in a surly way. "I don't have all day."

The secretary looked relieved that she didn't have to throw him out. He'd been so persistent earlier trying to get in to see Keegan. He followed her into the reception area, where he overheard another young woman say to the receptionist, "He wants the number of that air charter outfit."

"I guess I'll leave him a note," said Caruso, grabbing a memo pad from behind the front desk. As he scribbled in an irritated way, he watched the receptionist flip through the Rolodex, pick out a card, and hand it over her shoulder. He didn't get the number, but he got the name. Worthington Air Charters.

"Oh, never mind," he said, wadding up the note and flinging it at the desk. He turned on his heel and stalked out.

It was just a bit of luck that the red Mercedes was parked right in front. He knew whose it was because it had a vanity plate that said "Keegan." It was only a moment's work to pop the hood, pull the wires from the distributor cap, and slam the hood back down.

He checked his watch. Ten minutes ought to do it. He waited nine, then called Worthington.

"I'm calling from Trevor Keegan's office," he said. "Did someone just call you about a float plane?"

"Yes, they did. It'll be ready at our Hayward dock as soon as Mr. Keegan gets here," said an efficient-sounding woman.

"Well, there's been a change in plans," said Caruso. "Can you meet him at the dock outside Candlestick Park on this side of the Bay?"

There was a trace of irritation in her voice. "All right."

"Of course, we'll pay extra for that hop across the water," he added in a friendlier voice.

His car was back at the office. That was all right, because he wanted to stop off there first, anyway. He stepped into the middle of the street and flagged a cab. In his office, he swooped past Gail, told her breathlessly he was leaving town for the rest of the day, and went into his inner office. There he picked up the papers Ken Chavez had sent over by messenger, and the gun and ammunition he kept in his office safe.

Rebecca pulled back the bedspread and the worn wool blankets on the bed in her little cabin, and slid, fully clothed, between sheets that smelled like laundry soap with a touch of mildew.

She curled up, pulled the blankets over her, and felt her whole body relax. She had never known fatigue like this. It penetrated right into her bones, giving her a heavy, leaden sensation. For the first time in days, she felt relatively safe. There was nothing to do now but wait.

But now that she had time to reflect, she worried. How long would Keegan take to get here? Would Benjamin escape before that? She should have called the police. She hadn't been thinking. She was afraid of the police, afraid of being arrested. But if Benjamin came to and escaped — she knew she'd have to get up, get out of bed, and tell someone about Benjamin. They'd have to believe her. But before she could decide how to tell her story and to whom, she sank, quite suddenly, into a deep, dreamless sleep.

It had been remarkably easy. The pilot hadn't questioned him. After Caruso had boarded the plane and it had taken off, he looked down at the Bay Bridge. With a smirk, he imagined Keegan, driving perhaps a commandeered Toyota belonging to one of his secretaries, tryng to make it to Hayward.

There was always a chance Keegan would call Bill's Resort and tell them not to cooperate with anyone else who came looking for the woman, but he didn't think Keegan would do that. It might make Bill nervous and more likely to call the sheriff. Keegan, it was clear, didn't want any hick sheriff involved. He wanted to bring her back himself, preferably with full press coverage.

Then he'd try to get her into a mental hospital. Whether he planned to use her mental state as a defense in a new trial or as a ploy to get her out of prison and into some kind of treatment, Caruso wasn't sure. What he guessed was that Keegan probably did believe she was insane — whatever that meant. In any case, he believed that she'd killed Benjamin Knapp. Maybe he'd defended so many guilty people, he'd forgotten that there were some innocent ones out there too.

But then Caruso chided himself for jumping to conclusions. He wasn't sure she was innocent. He just knew it was possible, and he was going north to learn the truth.

27

When she woke up, it took a few seconds to realize where she was, although she associated this room with its low ceiling, old-fashioned maple furniture, plaid cushions and curtains, and vague, woodsy smell with a feeling of safety.

Then she remembered how she had come here, and in remembering Benjamin, the feeling of safety faded a little. She was awake now, growing more alert, because someone was knocking on the door. She heard the voice of Bill, the owner of this place. "Your friend from San Francisco's here," he called out. "Are you in there?"

"Yes," she called eagerly, and flinging back the covers, went to the door and drew back the chain. She could hardly wait to tell Keegan all that had happened, although she knew it would take a while to get her story across to him.

When she opened the door, her face was lit up and eager. But as soon as she saw Caruso standing there, it registered fear and confusion. Before she had a chance to say anything, Caruso stepped between her and Bill. "I guess you're surprised to see me," he said smoothly. "There's been a little change in plans, and we should talk about it."

"But Keegan — ," she began and turned to Bill. "This isn't Mr. Keegan," she said.

Caruso reached into his pocket and took out one of Keegan's cards, handing it to Bill. "I'm an associate of Mr. Keegan's," he explained. "The young lady and I will be back at the main lodge in a few minutes to settle the bill," he said, keeping his gaze pointedly on the man until he shoved the business card in his shirt pocket and left.

"What the hell are you doing here?" Rebecca said, pushing some of her tangled hair back from her face.

"I want to know what you're doing here," he said urgently. "How did you get here? Is Benjamin alive?"

"Yes," she said, with a huge sense of relief. "Oh, yes. He's alive. How did you know?"

"I hoped — I guessed."

She became wary again and stepped back from him. "What are you doing here? Where's Keegan? How did you know I was here?"

He put a hand on her elbow and guided her

back into her cabin. "Sit down," he said. "We just have a little time, I'm betting, until Keegan shows up." He closed the door behind them, but she didn't sit. "I'm here because I want to help you," he continued. "I don't believe you killed Benjamin, but I'm afraid no one else will believe you."

"First you turn me in to the police, now you say you want to help me. Are you crazy? And how did you find me?" She stared at him with her eyes wide.

"Never mind all that," he said. "I want you to take me to Benjamin. If Keegan gets here, he might not believe you. Rebecca, he's bringing a psychiatrist with him. They want to get you off on a psycho thing. Is Benjamin anywhere near here?"

"He's in the woods. Up a road. He took me there. Kept me there. I got away."

"How?"

"I hit him hard with a skillet. And then I gave him a shot."

"A shot?"

"The kind he gave me. Some kind of a sedative to keep me quiet." She rubbed her arm at the memory.

He glanced down at her gesture than back up at her face. "Are you all right? Did he — ?"

She turned away. "Rape me? He might

have wanted to, but I don't believe he could have."

"Thank God for that," said Caruso, staring at her back as she bent her head and shook with tears.

"Well I suppose I should be thankful," she snapped between sobs, "but I'm not. I feel like I've been through absolute hell. He abducted me and dragged me away and locked me up. And no one believed me. I'm going to prison — " She began to cry. He went over to her and reached out, then drew back before he touched her.

"I want you to take me to Benjamin," he said.

"I can't go back there."

"I'll be with you."

"I'm supposed to wait for Keegan." She straightened up and turned around to face him. "Why should I trust you? Why are you here? What do you want? It was you who got me into this mess in the first place."

"I just told the cops what I knew," he said.

"I don't want to take any more chances with you."

He went over to her and took her by the shoulders. "You have to. I'm the only person in the world who believes you," he said. "Besides," he smiled, "I'm arresting you."

"What?"

"A citizen's arrest. I've got a copy of the fugitive warrant from Ken Chavez, along with the forfeiture of bail notice. These papers say you're a fugitive. I'm working for him, and he's paying me to take you back to the jurisdiction of the Alameda County Court."

"This is ridiculous," she said.

"But before I take you back there, I want to find Benjamin." His hands still on her shoulders, he brought his face closer to hers. "Rebecca, it's your only chance. How long ago did you leave him there, and how far away is it?"

"If you're arresting me," she said coldly, "you can't force me to walk into the forest looking for Benjamin, can you?"

"No, I suppose I can't." He released her and stepped back. "But I'm asking you to take me to Benjamin voluntarily. I want you to trust me."

"Why should I trust any man again?"

"All right, Philip was worse than useless, and now Keegan's going to try and get you committed. You were wrong to trust them. But you've got to trust me."

"Why?"

"Because I want to find Benjamin. I want to set this all right. I've been involved ever since I found all that blood. Ever since you came to my office that day. I feel a responsibility to see it all end properly."

"So your professional pride is on the line?"

"Sure." He shrugged as if to indicate that was self-evident.

"And how do you know Keegan's coming here with a psychiatrist?"

"I was in his office when you called. I heard the whole thing on the extension. He's planning to bring up a Dr. Greenberg to check you out on the plane back."

"That's the name of the man he wanted me to see before," she said.

"Then," he added, "he wants a full-scale press conference with him as the star and you as the poor, distraught hysteric. We've got to hurry. He'll be here any minute. I'm not letting him have you. You're my prisoner, but it'll be a whole lot easier if we leave now."

"I'm so confused."

"Just trust me." He smiled at her. "After all, I'm trusting you. I believe you when you tell me Benjamin is alive."

Her face seemed to soften a little, then he cocked his head and held up a hand to silence her. "Quiet," he said. "Hear that? It's a helicopter. I bet Keegan's on it."

"We'll have to explain to him. The police should go get Benjamin. We can't — "

"Come on," he said a little roughly. "We've talked enough. Are you going to show me

Benjamin or am I just going to take you back to jail?"

"I'll show you Benjamin," she said.

28

As they walked back up the road that led away from the resort, he made her tell him everything that had happened. She told him about the van and the newspaper clipping and being locked in the room. She even told him she'd tried to kiss Benjamin and that he'd slapped her and called her a fucking slut. She told him about the way Benjamin liked his eggs, and how she'd stood over him, wondering whether to crush his skull with the skillet.

"I don't think I would have hesitated," he said.

"Have you ever been on trial for murder?" she said. "It's a real deterrent."

"I was astonished they found you guilty," he said. "Juries are hard to figure."

"They didn't believe Philip did it, I guess," she said. "If you didn't believe Philip did it, you'd have to convict me."

"But I never thought Philip did it either. All I could tell, sitting there in court, was that there was one person in the case crazy enough to have done it, and that was Benjamin himself. He was the only element in the case that fit in with the crime. But he couldn't have killed himself and removed his own body."

She sighed. "He tried to frame me. He thought I'd run away and be forced to stay with him. He didn't tell me how he managed to leave that crime scene there. He must have switched labels at the clinic or something. He was very cagey about that part. God, I wonder whose blood it was. Could it have been from a cadaver?"

"It was his," said Caruso. "I'm sure of it. He exfused it over a period of time and stored it. Froze it. Nothing to it, really. Body-builders do it all the time. They store their own blood and infuse it later. They call it blood doping. It doesn't require much skill. Leaves needle marks, though. That was my first clue. Benjamin had needle marks."

She fell silent, thinking about this for a while. "Then he planned it over a long period of time." She turned to him. "Do you have proof?"

"No. The best proof is Benjamin himself."

"I shouldn't have left him there. I should have called the police. I wasn't thinking."

"You've done pretty damn well, if you ask me. You got away. That's the main thing.

And don't worry. It may all work out better this way."

As they trudged along, she found herself amazed at the strength she still had. That deep sleep had done her some good. But her mind still reeled. Why was she going along with Michael Caruso? Weren't they crazy to go back there? She felt safe with Caruso, but still —

"I shouldn't have said I'd come with you," she said now.

"But you're under arrest," he replied. "Now tell me about the cabin. Do you remember the layout?"

"A big room as you go in. Then a bedroom off that, the room he kept me in. The kitchen's visible from the living room. And there's another bedroom at the far end of the living room."

"Is he armed?"

She looked startled. "No, I don't think so. I didn't see anything when I was looking for the keys."

"And the van's still there. We can take that." He seemed to be thinking aloud.

"What are we going to do when we get there?" she said. She hadn't even thought about that. She'd just wanted another human being to see Benjamin alive. "The van's no good," she added. "I couldn't find the keys."

"I can hot-wire it if I have to."

"But what are we going to do when we get there?" she persisted.

"You need a witness. If Benjamin's still there, I'm going to take a good long look at him. From then on, don't worry about it. You've been through a lot. I'll do the thinking."

"That's what Benjamin said. I shouldn't have come."

"We had to come as soon as we could and before Keegan got here. Benjamin can disappear again, you know."

"God, I hope he's still on the kitchen floor where I left him. I should have tied him up."

When they arrived at the clearing in front of the cabin, the van was still there.

"Oh God, I'm so scared," she said. The sight of the clearing and the cabin had set her shivering.

He put his arm around her. "Was there any other vehicle around here?" he whispered.

"I don't think so."

"Then he's probably here." Keeping his eye on the cabin door, Caruso walked to the front of the van and felt under the bumper. Then he went to the side of the car and felt in the space above the left rear tire. He showed Rebecca a small magnetic box. "I found the keys," he whispered. "How about getting in that van and locking it up tight? You'll be safe. Then I'll search the house."

She shook her head. "He might have another set of keys. Don't leave me. Not even for a minute. I can't let him get me again." She clung to his sleeve. "Please. I can't take any more."

"Can you come into the house with me? Show me where you left him. Maybe he's still there."

"You won't let him get me?"

He reached inside his jacket and took out his gun. "I won't let him get you," he said.

She turned her face away from the gun. "You've put me back in danger," she said. "Please, take me away. Please. I'm legally your prisoner. You can't make me do anything dangerous."

As she spoke, he'd been scanning the scene. "We've got to go check the kitchen," he said. "We've come this far."

She clung to him, weeping, as they approached the house. He pushed the door open with his foot and walked into the main room, his eyes moving all the time as he proceeded toward the kitchen. The house was eerily silent.

In the kitchen, she saw fried eggs splattered across the floor where they'd flown out of the pan, and the two castiron skillets on the floor next to the empty syringe. But Benjamin wasn't there.

She could hardly breathe now. "Please take me away," she whispered, sure Benjamin was watching and listening.

Caruso looked at the kitchen table. There, sitting next to the breakfast dishes, was an open box of .22-caliber ammunition.

She followed his gaze and stifled a scream.

"Okay," he whispered into her hair, "we're going now. Take it nice and easy. We're going to the van."

"We have to go," she said. "Don't lock me in that van. Please."

"Don't worry," he said. "Just keep walking. I'm right here and I've got a marksmanship medal from the police academy."

As soon as they cleared the house, she broke free and ran toward the van. He ran after her, and pushed her against the side of it. "Just stay here, and I'll find him," he whispered urgently. "He's somewhere around here, I know it. You won't be free until we get him." He scanned the area, paying particular attention now to an old shed that stood about twenty feet away on concrete blocks.

"But if he kills you then I'll be alone with him again," she said desperately. They were still whispering, but now, to her amazement, Caruso grabbed her by her upper arm, twisted it behind her, and spoke in a loud voice, almost a shout.

"I don't see anyone here. I don't believe Benjamin Knapp's alive." He opened the van door, and as he was bundling her in, his gun pointing to the sky, he added, "You're my prisoner. I'm taking you back to Alameda County. But seeing as you're the best-looking woman I've ever arrested, we'll stop at a nice romantic spot on the coast first. The Inn at the Cliffs. You'll love it."

He bounded in after her, put the key in the ignition, and took off down the road, closing the driver's door after they were underway.

"What are you talking about?" Rebecca screamed. "You're as crazy as Benjamin."

"Benjamin was watching us," said Caruso, shouting over her screams. "I saw his feet. He was standing in that shed. It was up on concrete blocks, and I saw his feet underneath it. He might have been armed, and you were right, he might have killed me and then you'd have been alone with him. We couldn't take that chance."

"What was all that about the Inn at the Cliffs?"

He laughed. "I wanted to make sure Benjamin didn't disappear into the woods. Nothing should get him motivated as much as the thought of you with another man." She stared at him, and he turned away from the wheel a second to look back at her. "You didn't think I was really going to — "

"After fifteen years of Benjamin Knapp," she said coldly, "I can be forgiven for believing anything is possible."

"I told you to trust me," he said.

"We've got to get the police."

"You want to take your chances with the local sheriff? Maybe he'd have the skill to get Benjamin out of those woods without scaring him off. But you might be sitting in a jail cell waiting to find out. They might not like my taking so long to get you back to Alameda County. For sure, they'd call Oakland, and those guys would be up here in a shot to take you back in handcuffs.

"Then Keegan and Dr. Greenberg would get into the act. Believe me, you're freer as my prisoner than you'd be if we let anyone else in on this. In all the scrambling for you, Benjamin wouldn't have any trouble slipping away, and no one would believe he was still alive."

"But you saw Benjamin's feet," she said. "You're a witness."

"Feet? You think they'll overturn a guilty verdict because I saw some feet?"

"I don't know what to do."

"Just let me decide," he said. "Benjamin

307

will find us, and we won't be on his terrain. I can get him for you. You need him to set you free."

29

She had grown weary of thinking. It seemed so tempting to do as he said and let him do the thinking for her. They drove down the logging road, bumpy and dusty. By the time her heart had finally stopped pounding and regained its own rhythm they had turned onto two-lane blacktop, leading to the highway heading south. She found herself staring out of the window, looking at trees and cars and road signs as if she'd just been born. After those days of isolation, the sights of the outside world seemed intense and profound, fascinating, yet evoking a strange melancholy.

She intentionally didn't look at Michael Caruso. If she did, she knew she'd begin worrying again, weighing all the possibilities, all the dangers.

Finally he spoke, and she turned to look at his profile. A strong nose with just a hint of a bump at the bridge, a heavy, dark brow, curly eyelashes above the flat plane of his cheekbone.

"You all right? You're so quiet."

"I don't know. I don't know anything any more." She leaned against the window and closed her eyes.

"Did he feed you? Are you hungry?"

She was startled. "Yes," she said. "Come to think of it, I *am* hungry."

He turned to her for an instant and smiled. "Good. That's a good sign. You're ready to join the living."

"He fed me bologna sandwiches and fruit cocktail — children's food."

"We can do better than that. You need red meat to build yourself back up. We'll order a good dinner."

"Eat, drink, and be merry," she said. "And then what will happen?"

"It will all end," he said. "I promise you."

"It'll never end," she said hopelessly. "Whenever I thought it had ended, it started again."

"This time," he said firmly, "it will end."

It was dark when they pulled into the circular drive of the Inn at the Cliffs. It was a long, tastefully bland rambling structure of low gray-stained cedar buildings hugging the ground. The rooms opened directly onto natural-looking landscaping — wind-pruned conifers and rough grasses — dramatically lit with amber-colored lights here and there, all leading to spectacular rocky cliffs with the Pacific audibly crashing and boiling below.

"I'm going to check in," he said. "Lock the doors to the van if you feel insecure. If I bring you in to the office, you might be recognized. Besides," he added, smiling a little at her tousled hair, "you look like hell."

Waiting for him, she felt the old panic returning. She watched him through the office windows, smiling, affable, flashing a credit card, signing the register. It seemed to take forever, and the song of crickets outside and the occasional metallic click of the cooling engine sounded loud and vaguely malevolent.

When he came back, they drove to one of the rooms far away from the office, and he let them in with his key. It was luxurious looking compared to the rather austere exterior, with peacock blue bedspreads on twin double beds, gray carpet, a huge television set, and short, fat chairs upholstered in hot pink. Everything was dimly lit by huge shaded lamps on low tables.

He locked the door and pulled the chain, then fell into one of the pink chairs. "We'll have some time," he said. "He'll have to walk or hitchhike out of there."

"What makes you so sure he'll come?" she said.

"He'll come."

She wanted to complain to him that he should have taken care of Benjamin up there. Shot him through the doors of the shed. Waiting like this was ridiculous. Then she remembered how she'd pleaded with him to take her away, terrified that Benjamin would kill him and she'd be alone with Benjamin again.

He picked up the phone on the table next to him, asked for room service, and loosened his tie. She noticed for the first time that he was wearing a gray silk suit in a coarse weave and a red tie. She looked down at her own dirty jeans and sweater — the outfit Benjamin had dressed her in. She hadn't changed it in days. She hadn't wanted to be undressed for an instant in that cabin. She knew he could come in any time and she'd felt so vulnerable.

"What do you think," Caruso was saying now as she walked nervously around the room, "prime rib and a big salad? Maybe a baked potato."

"All right," she said vaguely. "Medium rare."

"You should have some red wine too," he added. "You look pale. You might be anemic. My grandmother says red wine builds up the blood."

"Your grandmother?" she said dubiously, pausing in front of a big dresser mirror.

"She's ninety-four," he said "She must know something."

Her reflection frightened her. She did look pale, and there were circles under her eyes. Her face wasn't even clean, and her hair was a mess. She raked at it with her fingers.

He hung up and watched her in the mirror with apparent interest. She caught his eye and stopped fiddling with her hair, shrugged, and said, "You're right, I do look like hell."

He seemed to find this amusing, or endearing in some way, which irritated her. Men wanted to think that women were always fussing with themselves — because of men, presumably.

"Why don't you take a hot bath or a shower or something? It'll make you feel better," he said. "Dinner won't be here right away."

She thought about it for a second and realized how skittish she still felt. Then she remembered the bathroom door would lock. That would make her feel safe.

The little samples of soap and shampoo and hand lotion in the bathroom seemed like incredible luxuries, as did the hot water and thick white towels. She scrubbed at herself over and over again, wanting to wash off any trace of the time she'd spent with Benjamin.

Then, wrapped in towels, she sponged off her dirty sweater and jeans. She hated getting back into them, but at least her body was clean, pink from scrubbing and the hot water, and her clothes were warm and steamy from having hung next to the shower.

She came out of the bathroom rubbing her hair with a towel and feeling weak from the steam and lay down on one of the beds. Caruso had his jacket off. The sleeve buttons of his white shirt were undone and the cuffs rolled back. The sight of his gun and holster alarmed her, but comforted her at the same time.

"Why are you doing this?" she said, draping the towel around her neck, and propping herself up against the headboard with pillows fished out from beneath the peacock blue bedspread.

He paused a while, looking at her before answering. "I thought it was because I got you into this mess and I owed it to you to get you out."

"You thought?"

"Well I didn't really get you into this mess," he said. "Benjamin Knapp did."

"I still don't quite understand."

"Maybe it's because I don't trust anyone else to do the job right. I'm good at this kind of thing."

"Saving people?"

"Taking care of trouble. That's why I

314

wanted to be a policeman."

"You mean you're brave?"

"I can read people, I think fast, and my adrenaline works right. It's there when I need it. That's what it takes to be a good cop. It's just a set of skills. Like you're a scholar. It's the way we were made."

"But you're not a cop anymore," she said.

He smiled. "I wanted to choose my own cases. And the paperwork was a killer."

There was a knock at the door. He put his jacket back on, glanced behind the curtains for a moment, then let in a waiter with a rattling tray, who arranged everything on a table between the two pink chairs, accepted a tip, and left.

The sight of the food drove everything else from her mind. She sat while he poured her a glass of wine, then she ate eagerly, savoring each bite. He leaned back in his own chair, watching her, toying with his own food.

After a while, frowning in concentration as she sliced her meat, she said, "I still don't understand why you're here."

"Angela Casaretti says it's because I'm in love with you."

"What?" She stopped eating and stared at him, knife and fork suspended halfway between her mouth and her plate.

He shrugged and gave her a half smile. She

was surprised at the boyishness of the gesture, and she smiled back.

"Angela and I had lunch yesterday at the Italian place around the corner from our building. We talked about you."

"You did?" The idea of Angela and this man having lunch in a restaurant in San Francisco yesterday while she was locked up in Benjamin's cabin was somehow overwhelming. "You fell in love with me, so you decided to save me?"

"I didn't save you. You saved yourself. Remember?"

"But you kind of took over, didn't you?" she said, beginning to eat again, watching him over her fork. "Started deciding things for me. Why? By what authority?"

"Maybe Angela got it right," he said.

She frowned and looked away.

"You wouldn't like that, would you?" he said. "You probably don't want anyone to love you. Because of Benjamin."

"Perhaps," she said stiffly.

"Of all the things he's done, that would have to be the worst," he said.

She laughed. "How touching. You believe in love."

"That's right. Most people do."

"But does it make any sense?"

"Of course not. Love is" — he gestured and

316

gazed upward — "an act of faith.

"In fact, I remember from religion class in high school that one of the proofs of God's existence is that we yearn for him. Same thing. Everyone wants love, so it must exist."

"I think I can live without it," she said, attacking her potato.

"Yeah? Then what was Philip Patterson all about?"

"I was lonely. I guess I'll just have to get used to it."

"No you won't," he said. He added suddenly, "Besides, Philip was a jerk."

She sipped her wine and tried to act self-possessed. "It might have worked out if it hadn't been for Benjamin. It was too much for Philip. It would be too much for any man."

He just looked at her, his dark eyes softened with emotion.

"But you're here, aren't you?" she said irritably. "I suppose I ought to be grateful. But you can't expect to just say you love me and then . . . it's ridiculous."

"I don't expect anything," he said, "and yes, it's pretty ridiculous. I sat there in court day after day, and I fell in love with the back of your neck. What can I say?"

He reached across the table and touched the back of her neck underneath her wet hair.

"Don't," she said, throwing down her napkin and standing up. She turned away from him and instinctively put her own hand on the back of her neck, as if to shield it from his gaze.

"I'm sorry," he said, "I couldn't help it. I didn't mean to frighten you." He rose and stepped toward her. "I guess you think that what I might feel for you is what Benjamin felt."

She turned and glared at him. "That's right. It scares me."

"But it's not the same," he said urgently. "It can't be."

"What's the difference then?"

"The difference is I want you to want me as much as I want you."

She turned away again and said softly, "If I want you, it's for all the wrong reasons. Because I feel dependent and you make me feel safe. I'm so weak. I hate that."

"Why? Men want to make women feel safe. We can't help it, it's our nature," he said rather desperately. "And we need you as much. More. In ways that we can't describe."

"It's all so confusing," she said. "And it's all mixed up with the physical."

"That's right," he sighed. "It's definitely all mixed up with the physical."

She turned back to face him once again. "Stop being so condescending," she said.

"You seem to think you're an expert on relationships between the sexes and you're going to explain it all to me."

"Somebody might have to," he said, "because of Benjamin and what he's done to you. I'd like it to be me."

He took her face in his hands, while she stood very still, and he kissed her slowly.

Then the telephone rang.

30

They parted reluctantly and stood facing each other while he answered the phone.

"Hello."

"Mr. Caruso, this is Deputy Collins of the county sheriffs department." It was a typical cop's voice — patient, slow, firm, low, and calm. "We've been told you are harboring a fugitive. My partner and I are in the lobby here, and we'd like to come over and talk to you."

"I'll be right there," said Caruso.

He hung up. "The police. I guess someone recognized you. I'm going to the lobby to talk to them, and I'm pretty sure I can keep them out of here if they don't have a warrant. Anyway, I'll play it by ear. I don't want them to know you're here, and I don't want them to scare Benjamin off." He was slipping back into his jacket. "I'll take the key and let myself back in. Don't open the door for anyone."

She nodded. He could tell by her face she didn't want to be left alone.

"Look," he said, "I'll be right back. And I'm not going to let them take you. You're in my custody."

After he left he heard her slide the chain in place.

Caruso was halfway to the office when it dawned on him. He'd never heard Benjamin's voice. He'd always imagined a high-pitched whine, nothing like the calm voice on the phone. But he could be wrong. He turned and started to go back to the room. He saw the figure emerging from the shadows beneath a stairway for just a second before he felt the blow on the back of his head and fell, unconscious, to the gravel path. His arm was flung out to one side, and the room key fell just an inch from his open hand.

She was standing in front of the dresser mirror, pushing a wave into her hair, when she heard the key in the lock. Relieved and smiling, she sprang to release the chain.

It was as if he had been leaning against it. As soon as the chain was released, the door flew open and Benjamin tumbled in. She had no chance to scream.

He had his arm wrapped around her neck, so that her throat was squeezed by the crook of his elbow, and from the corner of her eye she saw the blade of a knife. He was holding it vertically just within her range of vision and whispering in her ear, through her damp hair.

"You're just a cheap goddamn whore, aren't you?" he said. "What do you think you're doing in this place with that man? I know just what you are." Then he began to cry. "You've been such a disappointment to me," he said, "Damn, Rebecca, I gave up everything for you, and you're no good, you're just a cheap slut like Mother said. There's only one thing left, one way to salvage our relationship, to purify it, to make it what it should be."

She didn't say anything. There was nothing to say. She'd tried to reason with him before, and she never knew what would set him off.

"Come on," he said. "Come with me." He dragged her out into the dark, the blade of his knife touching her cheek. If she screamed now, she thought, he'd cut her to ribbons — like he'd cut up that green dress Philip had given her.

He dragged her out onto the path that led to the cliffs. "Remember, Rebecca," he said urgently. "Remember our first date. It was a place like this — a cliff overlooking the ocean. And you told me you loved me."

She felt the damp sea air, smelled the salt, listened to the crunch of her feet on the gravel. There was a breeze on her face and warm tears. This time, she thought, he'd kill her. Surrounding them was an expanse of grass, artfully lit with amber lights so that the trees growing here and there cast long shadows. Was this the last landscape she'd ever see?

There was a bench at the end of the path, a rustic wooden bench that faced out to the ocean. In front of it was a short barrier of heavy chain and concrete posts painted in shiny white enamel. He stepped over that and lifted her up over it with him. She deliberately hooked her tennis shoe under the chain, but he jerked her loose.

They stood about a foot away from the edge — crumbling rock with a smattering of lichen — and watched as, far below, swirling dark water licked into little spaces at the base of the cliff.

"We're going to jump," he said calmly, trying to pull her erect. "Together. It's the only way. I believe we will be reincarnated together. Maybe as twins. We'll always be together. People will come here for years and marvel at our love."

"No, Benjamin," she said, trying not to scream and alarm him. "No. We mustn't. Let's talk first. Can we sit down on that bench and talk about this?"

Suddenly, they heard Caruso's voice, shouting out across the grass, and his feet, running.

"Let her go, Benjamin," Caruso said calmly but loudly. "Just let her go."

Benjamin turned around and faced Caruso, but he didn't let go of Rebecca or the knife. She began to wriggle in Benjamin's grasp. She'd rather be stabbed than thrown over the edge. She could hear the waves crashing on the rocks below.

"We're going to do it," Benjamin was shouting back at Caruso. "We're going to die together."

Rebecca felt like a squirming child. She twisted slowly in his grasp, hoping he was distracted by Caruso, but he turned, his face just an inch from hers. "You aren't afraid, are you?" he said. "I'm not." He stood behind her and held her by the shoulders, extending his arms out until the top of her body hung over the edge of the cliff while her feet curled inside her shoes, clinging to the rock. "We can hold hands all the way down," he said.

"Benjamin, I'm not ready," she said, closing her eyes, but not before seeing the sheer rock wall beneath her and the huge, barnacle-encrusted rocks gleaming wetly below in the dim light.

He pulled her slowly back and maneuvered her over to one side. He had one arm around her and was facing Caruso. Benjamin's face was flushed and his eyes glittered. Rebecca realized with horror that he was quite happy. Happier than she'd ever seen him.

"Let her go," said Caruso. He walked slowly but purposefully toward them. Both hands were on his gun and his arms were extended. Behind him, she was dimly aware of other people, farther back.

She realized how close she was standing to Benjamin, and wished she could get clear. She tried to step sideways, but they were standing so near the edge that the slightest misstep would send her backward. She glanced over at Benjamin. He had his left arm around her and in the right, he still held the knife. He was showing it to Caruso.

"Put down the knife," Caruso said.

"Who cares about the knife?" said Benjamin gleefully. "I don't need it anymore. We're going over the edge. Together." He flung the knife over his shoulder, over the cliff into the water below.

The gesture necessitated his loosening his grip on her for just an instant, and Caruso shouted, "Rebecca, get down."

She wrenched herself away from him and fell onto the ground. She grabbed the chain barrier. Benjamin reached for her.

Caruso fired.

She twisted around and looked up at Benjamin. The impact of the bullet entering his body had blown him off the cliff. He seemed to hang in the air for just a moment, staring down at her, his mouth a startled O, and then he fell backward, his arms flopping helplessly. He didn't scream, so he must have been dead all the way down.

She clambered over the chain and fell back, collapsing against the base of the bench as Caruso came rushing toward her. In the distance, she could hear sirens. Below, she heard the waves, and above, the gulls.

Rebecca Kendall stood up in court, facing the judge. She wore a brand new red linen dress. He cleared his throat, looked down at her, and said: "In light of new evidence presented by the prosecution that Benjamin Knapp was not murdered, I hereby vacate judgment and dismiss this case." He leaned over and smiled. "You're free to go," he said.

Keegan patted her arm. She smiled at him. "A victory lunch, my dear?" he said. She didn't bother to point out that the victory wasn't his. "I've got other plans," she said. "But thanks anyway."

While he gathered up his papers, she turned, gave Keegan a perfunctory nod and walked out of the courtroom. Reporters and television newspeople were waiting for her in the hall, but she just kept walking, taking

326

long, purposeful strides down the courthouse steps.

When she saw Michael Caruso he was waiting at the curb, leaning on his car with his arms crossed in front of him, following her progress through the crowd. She smiled and quickened her pace. When she came to within a foot of him, she stopped.

He opened the door for her, went around to the driver's side, and drove away, leaving the press at the curb.

"I like your dress," he said.

"I never wore a red dress before," she said. "I guess I was afraid of attracting attention."

"You can wear all the red dresses you want from now on," he said.

She sighed and stretched, as if the car were too small for her expansive mood. "I'm free — completely. The judge said so too."

She frowned and looked at him. "But, Michael, I'm still sorting out what happened. I know we've been all through this, but I want to ask you again. Why did we leave Benjamin behind up in the woods? Why did we lure him out instead?"

"Because I saw that box of shells in the kitchen. I knew he had a shotgun. He could have killed us. Or me, and you'd have been alone with him again. I couldn't take a chance that he'd burst out of that shed firing."

"But if you knew he was armed, wasn't it dangerous to lure him to the inn? Anyone could have been hurt."

"I figured he couldn't hitchhike or wander down the highway with a shotgun without attracting attention." He was answering as if by rote or from a catechism.

"But why didn't we call the police from the inn? They could have caught him coming after me."

"Because, first of all, they might not have believed us. Second, they might have scared him off. And third — "

"Yes?"

With apparent reluctance, and in a new tone, he said, "Well, to tell you the honest truth, I figured that if they were involved, they might take him alive. Then you'd have never been free."

"Michael, you wanted to kill him, didn't you?" Her voice was strangely flat, as if she meant to strip the idea of its horror.

"As long as he was alive, you'd never be free — you'd never be free to want to wear a red dress or to let someone love you." He said it very firmly, but turned to look at her with a flicker of uncertainty, as if fearful of her disapproval.

"I see." She stared at him for a second, then turned away and said thoughtfully, "It was so dangerous. Were you thinking completely logically?"

He smiled. "Absolutely not. Any more questions?"

She looked out the window as he maneuvered the car onto the Bay Bridge.

"Yes. Where are we headed?"

"I don't know," he said. "You decide. I'll take you anywhere you want to go."